Nationwide praise for <u>CURIOUS WINE</u>:

"How many of us out there have been waiting with bated breath for the ultimate lesbian love novel to appear, complete with authenticity in plot and characters, and fine quality writing? Look no further, sisters, because the long-awaited jewel has arrived with <u>CURIOUS WINE</u>."

<u>THE LESBIAN NEWS</u>, Los Angeles

"I can't imagine anyone's not enjoying this engaging account of two beautiful women discovering themselves and each other. Forrest's offering is beautifully written, fast-paced, and more than mildly erotic."

<u>GLC VOICE</u>, Minneapolis

"Katherine Forrest writes with such feeling, passion and beautiful detail, that <u>CURIOUS WINE</u> is a masterpiece of lesbian love."

<u>THE SACRAMENTO STAR</u>

"The focus of the novel is love: falling in love, being in love, running away from love . . ."

<u>THE ADVOCATE</u>

"BOOM—the book ended. I wanted more . . ."

<u>NEWS JERSEY</u>

"Descriptive adjectives would be superfluous in relating one's impressions after having read this beautiful, tenderly touching love story. It rings a responsive chord in those of us who are romantic, revel in the erotic as powerful, and who enjoy a good, intense book."

<u>THE WISHING WELL</u>

"Subtly, beautifully, with unerring feeling not only passion but emotion and rationale are limned. A story about two adults, surprised by life but going to meet it head on, is a joy . . ."

<u>MOM GUESS WHAT</u>, Sacramento

"The lushness and sensual tone of <u>CURIOUS WINE</u> stirs the imagination. Ms. Forrest has created a milestone of a novel . . ."

<u>B.A.D. NEWS</u>

". . . a beautifully written intensely romantic fantasy . . . This novel is great for escape and difficult to put down until you have finished it . . ."

<u>GAZE</u>, Memphis

WORKS by KATHERINE V. FORREST

CURIOUS WINE

Katherine V. Forrest

The Naiad Press, Inc.
1997

Printed in the United States of America
First Edition
First Printing—May 1983
Second Printing—June 1983
Third Printing—March 1984
Fourth Printing—March 1986
Fifth Printing—June 1988
Sixth Printing—August 1989
Seventh Printing—July 1991
Tenth Anniversary Edition
First Printing—April 1993
Second Printing—April 1994
Third Printing — January 1996
Fourth Printing — April 1997

Cover design by Catherine Hopkins
Typeset by Sandi Stancil

All of the poetry quotations are from *The Complete Poems of Emily Dickinson,* edited by Thomas H. Johnson (Little, Brown and Company).

Poem #1473 by Emily Dickinson on page 44 as well as a portion of Poem #599 on page 18 are reprinted by permission of the publishers and the Trustees of Amherst College from *The Poems of Emily Dickinson,* edited by Thomas H. Johnson, Cambridge, Mass.: The Belknap Press of Harvard University Press, Copyright © 1951, 1955, 1979 by the President and Fellows of Harvard College.

Poem #1654 by Emily Dickinson on page 23 as well as a portion of Poem #599 on page 18 are from *The Complete Poems of Emily Dickinson,* edited by Thomas H. Johnson. Copyright © 1914, 1929, 1942 by Martha Dickinson Bianchi; Copyright renewed 1957 by Mary L. Hampson. Reprinted by permission of Little, Brown and Company.

Library of Congress Cataloging-in-Publication Data

Forrest, Katherine V., 1939–
    Curious Wine.
    I. Title.
PS3556.0737C8   1993 813'.54   82-24663
ISBN 1-56280-053-1

About the Author

Katherine V. Forrest is a naturalized citizen who was born in Canada, in 1939. She has lived in the East, the Pacific Northwest, and the far West. She has held management positions in business, and is now writing full time and living in San Francisco.

For Sheila
Who has made everything possible

I had been hungry, all the Years —
My Noon had Come — to dine —
I trembling drew the Table near —
And touched the Curious Wine —

— Emily Dickinson

The cabin was warm and bright with the light Diana Holland and Vivian Kaufman had seen from a distance on the winding mountain road, friendly yellow light radiating into a black night, onto glowing snow.

Liz Russo greeted them with shouts of welcome, a flurry of hugs for Vivian, a collecting of coats. Four other women were gathered around a huge blazing fireplace; one arrested Diana's attention immediately. She sat on the hearth, and rose as Liz Russo introduced all the women.

Lane Christianson, the woman Diana had noticed, extended a hand to Diana and then to Vivian. Tall and slender, she pushed blonde hair back from her forehead.

"Elaine?" Vivian said, smiling and holding her hand for a moment before releasing it.

"Lane," she corrected. "Short for Mar-lane-a, as in Dietrich. My mother was a big Dietrich fan and she didn't stop to think how inconsiderate it was to give me three syllables in each name."

"Lane is nice," Vivian said, smoothing and straightening the jacket of her plaid pantsuit.

Perfectly fitting deep green pants and a camel sweater clung softly to Lane Christianson. Diana, having already tidied her own sweater over her pants, reflected with amusement than an unusually attractive woman always seemed to make other women self-conscious, slightly defensive. She glanced at her admiringly but curiously; the other women wore jeans and sweaters or sweatsuits.

"I suppose I should be grateful for Marlene. Mother might've been a bigger fan of Hedy Lamarr or Pola Negri," Lane said to Vivian. "What could you do with Hedy or Pola?"

The women laughed, and Lane smiled; to Diana the smile seemed cool, remote.

Vivian said, "Do all of you know Liz's maiden name?"

"Sure. Taylor," said Madge Vincent.

Diana said, chuckling, "You used to be Liz Taylor?" Lane laughed, a light silvery sound.

"Damn you, Kaufman," Liz said, "I ought to pull your false eyelashes off." She said ruefully to Diana, including Lane in her glance, "Imagine growing up with a name like Liz Taylor. I wanted to get married when I was twelve just to get rid of it."

The women laughed. Liz asked Diana, "What would you like to drink? We're out of vodka but there's lots of bourbon and scotch and gin. A little wine, too."

"Wine, if it's white."

"It's white, but not exactly what they serve at the Beverly Hilton. My sons keep it here. Make yourself comfortable, dear. If you don't like the wine you can join the drinkers. Viv, come on in the kitchen honey, let's bullshit."

The fireplace was surrounded by a long sofa, two armchairs, and a circular coffee table with drinks and a tray of cheese. Large corduroy cushions were scattered over a raised hearth. Diana decided to sit near the fire.

Madge Vincent said, "May we assume you and Vivian have a good reason for wanting to live in your awful city?" An intense-looking woman of perhaps thirty-five, with disheveled shoulder-length dark hair, she sat on the sofa tapping her cigarette into an ashtray overflowing with long cigarette butts.

Diana settled herself on a cushion, smiled and extended her hands in a conciliatory gesture. "I bow to the superiority of your beautiful city. Especially since I'll be outnumbered five to one when Viv leaves. It's not really my fault, though. I can't help it if I was born there. In beautiful downtown Burbank, in fact."

Chris Taylor said, "You knew Viv was born in San Francisco, didn't you?" She was slightly pudgy, with graying hair and timid, anxious blue eyes. Diana had learned from the introductions that she was Liz's sister.

"Yes. I've heard lots of stories about you and Liz and Viv all growing up together. I finally got to meet Liz a year ago Christmas. She came down with her husband for the holidays." She smiled, remembering how much she had liked the Kaufmans: Liz, big and physical and warm-hearted; and her husband, a loud cigar-smoking gentle bear of a man.

"You heard they got divorced."

"Yes, Viv told me. I felt very bad."

"Twenty years." Chris sighed. "We don't mention George around Liz."

Diana watched Millie Dodd, who sat cross-legged on the floor, lift from a well-padded case a guitar which had the high gloss of expensiveness, and lay it across her knees. "George and Millie," she intoned in a hushed whisper, and struck the strings with an abrupt slash of her fingers, producing a dramatic thrumming of finality. She pushed at chemical blonde hair, a frizzy cloud around her face, and smiled in delight at her musical effect, blue eyes as ingenuous as a child's. Diana thought she could be as young as twenty-five, as old as forty.

Millie continued a low pleasant strumming as Liz brought Diana her wine and returned to the kitchen. Diana sipped from the small heavy wine glass; with a shudder of distaste she placed it on the hearth and looked up to meet the amused eyes of Lane Christianson.

"Not exactly vintage."

"A tad too much vinegar," Diana joked, noticing an identical glass, almost full, beside her.

"More like the whole vinegar bottle. Maybe you'd like liquor."

"I only like vodka."

"Me too."

"I'll get us something when I'm out."

Diana's eyes lingered on Lane Christianson. Leaping firelight reflected gold highlights in her hair, which was shades of blonde and silk-textured, reaching just below the nape of her neck, framing her face and falling over her forehead. Cut in layers that shifted in pattern as she moved her head, her hair reminded Diana of a stand of autumn trees she had once seen in Utah with leaves like sunlit coins, blowing in the wind in changing colors of gold. In the firelight, the warm tones of her skin suggested the topaz she would become under a summer sun. Diana could not decide if her eyes were gray or blue. Lane sat relaxed, legs curled gracefully under her, but with her slender body erect and her shoulders very straight. Diana thought her beautiful.

"What do you do, Diana?" Millie asked.

"I'm a personnel representative for West Coast Title and Trust," Diana answered, turning reluctantly away from Lane to the other women.

"Do you work with their customers then?" Chris asked.

"No, I hire people. I work a lot with Viv. Do all of you know she's a supervisor? I've hired a lot of word processing people for her."

"Ever hire somebody she hates?" Chris asked.

Diana was amused by the question. "She hollers once in a while. I make good choices, usually."

"I imagine the worst problem is just keeping people on the job," Lane commented.

"Yes." Diana gazed at her again. "People drift from job to job, it's amazing. I interview people in their early twenties with a dozen jobs already, they see no reason why it should be any different." She asked with a prickling sense of expectancy, "What do you do?"

"I'm a lawyer."

"Good for you." She was gratified that this impressive woman had applied her intellect and physical gifts to a challenging profession.

"One nice thing about being in a group like this, I don't have to have the adjective for a change. When I work I'm always the woman lawyer. Out of earshot, I'm sure I get other adjectives."

The women chuckled. Diana asked, "Do you have your own practice?"

"I'm with a law firm. With five names. I'll give you a card if you think you might need help sometime." Her voice was light, her eyes animated.

"Do you specialize?"

"I work on the stupid messes our corporate clients get themselves into with civil rights violations."

"That's just great!"

"No, frustrating. Like trying to change the tides. We've had the Civil Rights Act since 'sixty-four, all the lip service anybody could ask for, all kinds of smoke and fire—and it's shocking, the little progress.

Bad as it is for women, it's worse for blacks—most management people I know want them to go back to picking cotton."

"I agree with you about women," Chris said, "but sometimes I wish—mind you I'm just as liberal as the next person, I just wish that's where the blacks had stayed. And those other people flooding into San Francisco these days, those . . . those . . ."

"Chris, get out of your time capsule," Madge said. "This is nineteen seventy-*eight*. People have got to allow other people their own space."

"That's easy for you to say, they're buying property like crazy, those . . . *perverts*."

"Chris—"

"Madge, I don't feel like arguing," Chris said.

"Neither do I," Lane said, her smile thin and tired. "I came up here to get away from all that."

Diana asked in the awkward silence, "Are you in real estate, Madge?"

"More or less. I'm kind of itinerant." She drew deeply from her cigarette and reached for the ashtray. "What all of you do is a lot steadier than my profession."

"I thought real estate was booming. It certainly is in Los Angeles."

"That's the trouble." Madge extinguished her cigarette and ran her fingers through her hair. She inserted another cigarette between thin lips and smiled sourly at Diana as she flicked a tiny gold lighter. "Everybody and his brother are into it. I happened to meet Lane when her firm handled a problem for my agency. She's a good lawyer, but she cares too much and works too hard."

"Real estate isn't my field," Lane said, looking at Diana. "I was helping a colleague, I had to research everything. Which made me a poor lawyer who took longer to get things done," she added with a chuckle.

"She got here two hours before you did," Madge said to Diana. "Has to leave Wednesday. She was supposed to drive here with me two days ago to relax and ski for a whole week."

"Last minute complications, Madge. It happens."

"All the time to you, Lane."

Diana said, "What do you do, Millie?"

"I'm a nurse," Millie said, sipping what appeared to be a martini. "Chris and I live just down the street from each other. She's not really quite so narrow-minded as she seems."

Chris said tartly, "I work for a vice-president of Shell. You ought to hear his opinions."

"How long have you been with Shell?" Diana asked, anxious to change the subject.

"Twenty-four years this past month."

"Really? It sounds like you have a very responsible position."

"I worked my way up to it. I've been a secretary all my life and I've never felt the least bit apologetic about it."

"Why should you, if it belongs in your script?" Madge said.

Diana smothered a smile. Liz and Vivian came out of the kitchen arm in arm, carrying drinks. Feigning polite interest in the continuing conversation, Diana examined her surroundings.

The fireplace, floor to ceiling slab stone, dominated the cabin dramatically, and the major furniture was clustered around it. Dark wood paneling was warm and lustrous, blending with the rich brown shag carpeting. A curved breakfast bar separated the kitchen from the main room. Diana thought that the kitchen seemed unusually well-equipped for a cabin, with generous-sized cupboards and counters, a large refrigerator, an elaborate stove. In the dining area a tiffany lamp hung over an oval table surrounded by wicker chairs. A bookcase held games and cards and puzzles, a collection of paperbacks, and a matched set of books, probably classics. Off the dining area was a doorway, apparently to the back bedrooms and bathroom. A sturdy ladder leaning against one wall led to an open trapdoor in the ceiling.

Diana peered up at the trapdoor, imagining the beauty of the snow and trees she could see from above. Pain, sudden and sharp, unexpected, stabbed at her. Jack . . . the strength and warmth of his arms with all this cold and snow around them . . .

She started as Lane said, "Wait'll you see it up there."

"Can you see much out the window?"

"Only the universe." She smiled, then shook her head. "Liz says nobody likes to climb the ladder with luggage, so cabin rules are, last to arrive has to sleep up there. You can't imagine how incredible it is."

Diana looked at the trapdoor again, with a surge of anticipation.

Lane said, "Do you want to take your luggage up and see it? I'll help."

"Diana honey," Vivian called. "Time to take Vivian to her awful fate."

Diana waved at her. "I have to take Viv into town," she said to Lane. "She's staying at Harrah's with a friend."

"She is? Why aren't they staying here? Oh, of course. The friend's of the male gender."

Diana smiled. "Exactly."

Lane shrugged. "I wanted to come up here and get away from all that for a while, too. We'll go up when you get back, then. Or are you going to stay and gamble?"

"No," Diana said, deciding immediately. "I'll be back."

Liz helped Vivian into her coat. "Let's get you to your den of iniquity, my dear. I'm sure John is so excited he's had to put on his baggy tweeds. Is he any good at all?"

"Good for hours," Vivian crowed, tugging playfully on a curly lock of Liz's hair, light brown and shot through with threads of gray.

"Bullshit! How would you know? You couldn't last fifteen minutes these days, you old bag." Liz poked Vivian in the shoulder.

"You want a screwing contest?" Vivian shouted. "You just let me know, you broken down old broad!"

Chris said resignedly, "Always they talk like that. Even when we were kids. Worse."

Diana shrugged into her jacket, smiling, noticing Lane's grin.

Vivian said, "Try to be nice to my Diana, Liz. She's a very delicate child these days."

Diana, furious, stared at Vivian.

"What do you mean, delicate?" Liz asked, looking from Diana to Vivian with amused, interested dark eyes. "Is she pregnant?"

Diana laughed in spite of herself, and Vivian said, with a soothing glance at her, "She just needs rest and relaxation from all the cares and worries." She addressed the group. "Will I see all of you again at the casinos?"

"We'll be in," Chris said.

Outside the cabin, Diana turned on Vivian. "How dare you do that to me. Liz I barely know, those other people are total strangers. I should've known better than to come up here, I knew this was a hare-brained—"

"Honey, I haven't said anything much —"

"Anything *much*? You talked to Liz on the phone, set this up. How *much* did you tell her?"

"Nothing much at all, honey." Vivian climbed into the car. "Don't be mad at Vivian who loves you. Just let yourself enjoy this, Diana. Isn't the cabin marvelous? God, I'd be enjoying that great fireplace and that fabulous view right along with you if it weren't for John being up here. And Liz, God love her. There's nobody quite like Liz."

"They're skiers," Diana said sulkily, slamming her car door. "They'll nag me to try it again. Skiers are like that. I *hate* skiers."

Vivian reached to her, took her hand. "If you really don't like them, really don't want —"

Diana squeezed her hand, released it. "I didn't say that. I just meant —"

"They seem like very nice people. That Lane's a knockout. If you like slim gorgeous women," she added humorously.

Diana chuckled. "She's a lawyer."

"God, even more disgusting."

Diana started the car. "Madge and Millie seem okay, but Chris — it gets harder all the time for me to be around intolerant people."

"Don't mind Chris. She's just a pathetic old maid, dried up inside and out. She was a boring old woman by the time she was nine, take it from Vivian. Too bad you won't try skiing just one more time. If I had your body I'd live in ski clothes. It's a better way to meet men than on a stupid golf course."

Diana said wearily, "I don't play golf anymore." She changed the subject. "God, it's black up here."

"You haven't played golf in six weeks, to be exact. You'll have to come out of the convent sometime, dearie. Just to take care of the bodily necessities. How long do you think you can go without sex?"

"Forever," Diana said grimly.

"Not you. You're not that kind of woman. You need somebody loving you."

"Wrong. After Tommy I didn't have sex or even want it for months and months, more than a year. The whole time I lived with Barbara. Everybody I dated got only the pleasure of my company." Diana squinted through the darkness, her headlights picking up walls of snow sheared into stratified layers by snow plows, and the symmetrical shapes of pine trees.

"Not wanting sex isn't a bit strange after what you went through with that drunk. I was like that after Joe the schmoe. But it's easier to do without in your twenties. Women need it more when they get older. Forty-two isn't such a bad age, either, I can tell you. Although I wouldn't mind being thirty-three again."

"Thirty-four."

"Thirty-four. You're so attractive. I don't even like to let you near John, if the truth be told. Though he tells me he prefers his women well-padded, thank God. I'll tell you now that it's over with Jack, at least I hope it's over, I don't know what you saw in that piece of male fluff. Good-looking, yes, but that's all. Not much wonder he's done everything but throw himself under the wheels of your car to get you back. He'll never have anything like you again."

"I don't want to talk about this anymore," Diana said evenly, steering the car carefully around the curves, watching for ice patches in the road.

"Anymore? You haven't talked about it at all. I don't know what you think friends are for. You've done your mourning for him, six weeks is more than he deserves. But no, nine hours to Tahoe and all I get is your long face. I felt like stopping the car and performing a mercy killing."

Diana laughed.

"That's better. Are you still taking the pill?"

"Yes Viv. Yes, mother."

"Jason at work is panting after you."

Diana shrugged.

"What's wrong with him?"

"He bores me."

"So why are you taking the pill, my little nun in a convent?"

Irritated, Diana did not answer.

"Well, it's intelligent, whatever your reason. You might meet someone up here."

"If I do, I don't intend to hop into bed with him."

"Phooey. I was in bed with John two hours after I met him."

Diana glanced at her friend in amusement. "John's lasted longer than any of your other . . . enthusiasms, I will say that."

"Why shouldn't I do what I feel like doing? All the men do. I've done my biological duty, I've produced a child. Now my vagina's strictly for fun. Nothing is forever, Vivian's learned that much after her two disasters. Wait'll you hear the joys of divorce San Francisco style from Liz. Twenty years, for God's sake. If I ever thought two people would go to the undertaker together it was Liz and George. Till George leaped out of his shorts over some hot blonde thing in his office. God, men can be such bastards, such pricks."

Diana had reached the intersection of Highway 50, and she waited for an opening in the Saturday night traffic streaming toward the casinos.

"You need a love affair, Diana. A good love affair."

Diana pulled onto the Highway. "I had one. Jack was more fun than anyone I've ever known. I never knew what he'd do next. He was like a man-child to me."

"I'm sure," Vivian said with ill-disguised sarcasm. "I mean a real love affair. Mind-blowing sex, all you do is go to bed and come till you're vanilla pudding."

Diana laughed. "Viv, you're bad."

Vivian grinned lasciviously. "It's good to be bad."

"I can't believe how built up it is now," Diana said, gazing at glittering blinking miles of neon along Highway 50.

"I always thought your feeling for Jack was more protective than anything else. I can't imagine him burning up the sheets."

Diana sighed. "You have a one track mind tonight."

"I'm just used to all your little tricks by now, how you change the subject."

"You're straying into private territory, that's all. I loved going to bed with Jack." She added affectionately, "I'm just not the blabbermouth you are."

"How would you know if he was any good? You've had precious little experience for this day and age."

"Viv, we've been through this before. I don't think experience is important. I just don't. I didn't need the three men before Jack to know how good it was with him." The dark tower of Harrah's came into view. She stared curiously; the hotel had been built since the last time she was here.

"Three *men*? Your marriage hardly counts. It's a wonder you didn't leave that drunken fool of a Tommy still a virgin. And that

McDonnell-Douglas engineer— At least tell me this, Diana. Was Jack that good in bed? Really?"

"Yes, for me. Really."

"Men are really good in bed when they want more than their own pleasure, when they really, really love women. That makes them sensitive."

"Jack was sensitive. He loved women."

"Was that it, Diana?" Vivian asked softly. "Were there other women?"

"I don't want to talk about it." Diana bit off the words.

"You're the most honest person I've ever known. Too honest, you never spare yourself anything. You're so quiet, you look so tired all the time—I know you've got to work this through but don't exhaust your strength when you have friends who love you and want to help."

"Thank you, Viv," Diana said, tears stinging her eyelids.

She knew she had no choice but silence. How could she explain, justify her feelings to anyone? There had to be something wrong with her. How else could she explain the coldness she had discovered in herself after five years of loving Jack Gordon?

She could not forgive him. After six weeks, she could not even consider forgiving him. Agonized by his absence, she had been sullen and waspish in his presence; he had called, rung the apartment buzzer, accosted her in the apartment garage and at her office. Her mind shuttered from him, angry at his hurt, she had refused to listen, turned away repelled when he tried to touch her. Every shred of feeling for this man she had loved better than any other in her life had vanished.

There was more evidence: You never wanted children, she accused herself. Yes, Tommy was a drunk, but that had been an excuse. She had been happy when Jack declared that he wanted only her; living with him unmarried had given her the excuse to avoid discussion or admission that she did not want children—that there was a cold and unloving core in her, that there was something wrong with her.

With Vivian's luggage in the care of a bellman, Diana kissed her cheek. "I'll see you tomorrow."

Vivian held her at arm's length. "Aren't you going to stay? And play? Say hello to John?"

"You and John will have your own hellos to take care of," Diana teased. "I'll be here in the morning."

"Liz won't have a phone in that place, she thinks she's roughing it. All it does is make things awkward."

"I'll find you, don't worry."

"Why not stay and play?" Vivian coaxed. "You can't meet—I mean, you've got to get out and around and—"

"The cabin was your idea, remember? If I'm going to be spending the next four days there, I'd better be a little sociable, don't you think?"

"You're right, honey. But get out of there as much as you can. Nothing interesting can possibly happen in a cabin full of women."

I s that what I hope it is?" Lane had walked into the kitchen.

Diana unpacked a paper bag. "Vodka . . . and this was the best of the wine they had chilled."

Lane inspected the two wine bottles. "Very nice. Good." She rummaged in a drawer for a corkscrew. "Which one do you want opened?"

"You choose. My father's the wine-lover. Anything I know, he taught me."

"Are you close to your father?"

"Yes. Very close." She watched Lane work the cork out with expertise.

"Why don't we take your luggage up now?"

"I've been looking forward to it."

With a brief word of explanation to the other women who were gathered around the fire animatedly talking, Diana picked up her bag and followed Lane, climbing the ladder with ease.

She stepped into a room filled with silver light from the window, illumination from the sky and snow. In the shadowy light she saw a brass bed, a sharply sloping ceiling, a small dresser and closet. Lane removed the glass from a kerosene lamp on the nightstand, struck a match to the wick. The pool of yellow light revealed details to Diana: a bright gingham quilt and fluffed up pillows, a circular braided rug, the raw wood of the ceiling.

"Turn out the light and come over to the window."

Diana blew out the lamp and the room again filled with silvery light. "Oh," she breathed as she reached the window.

The sky was spread with stars, a glittering endless carpet. Trees, stark and white with snow, stood fantastically against the sky. Snow lay in dramatic sculptures, huge drifts casting immense powerful shadows.

"Incredible," murmured Diana, circling Lane with an arm in an involuntary seeking of physical closeness in this icy grandeur.

They stood silent. Then Lane said, "It's good to share the newness of this as well as the beauty."

"You've never been here before?"

"No. Madge has asked me to come many times. She's the only one here I know."

Diana smiled. "Do you think you can resist the temptation to strangle Chris?"

Lane answered with an easy smile. "I meet Chrisses every day. But it'll be nice having someone around to change the subject."

"I'm good at it," Diana said wryly. "I suppose we'd better get down there and be sociable," she said regretfully, staring out the window, releasing Lane.

"Let me show you the rest."

A part of the pine wall slid back on a pulley system, revealing a narrow room with twin beds and a dresser.

Lane said, "Why don't we flip a coin for who sleeps where, and then alternate so we can both enjoy the big room?"

"Why should we do that, Lane? There's only a tiny window in here. That brass bed's queen-size. Do you snore?"

Lane grinned. "I've never had any complaints."

"Gnash your teeth? Kick? Sleepwalk? Then it's settled."

They climbed down the ladder. Liz watched them, hands on her hips. "Everything okay up there?"

"It's fantastic," Diana said.

Liz smiled thinly. "It's comfortable. Well-insulated, too. If you pull up the ladder and lower the trapdoor it holds the fireplace heat in pretty well all night. But turn the heater on if you get cold."

"How come we're so lucky?" Diana asked.

"Not so lucky. There's no john, you have to drag your luggage up, it's a pain in the ass."

"If I were you I'd sleep up there all the time."

"Millie," Liz said abruptly, "get busy and play something."

"Diana, I'll pour some wine," Lane said, eyeing Liz.

Millie strummed lightly and turned keys, adjusting the strings. Continuing to strum in a harmonic pattern, she sang "If I Were a Carpenter" in a thin pure voice, singing with clear simplicity.

Madge and Chris applauded.

"Hey Millie, that's beautiful," Diana said softly.

"Nice," Liz agreed.

"Really," Lane said.

"Anything you want to hear? What about you, Lane?"

"You're doing fine. Anything you want to sing."

"What about you, Diana?" Millie asked. "What kind of music do you like?"

"Sinatra, Ella, people like that. Peggy Lee is my favorite."

"How come somebody young as you likes such stodgy stuff?" Millie's tone was artless.

"It's classic stuff." Lane's voice was cold.

"Blame it on my father." Diana smiled at Millie. "He taught me to love stodgy people."

Lane said, "I have a wonderful Peggy Lee album I've never seen anywhere and believe me, I've looked. It's called *Pretty Eyes*."

Diana said incredulously, "You have that album? I've got it too! I've played it so much the grooves are almost worn through."

"Mine too, I've got it on tape now, so I feel a little more secure. One of the great Peggy Lee albums ever. Beautiful. Romantic."

"I'll just strum a few folk songs," Millie said grumpily.

Diana sipped her wine and studied the women. Liz, the sleeves of her maroon sweatshirt pushed up to the elbow, sat with a blue-jeaned leg hung over the arm of the sofa; she held an icy glass of dark brown bourbon. Next to her, Madge pulled at the skimpy ends of dark hair, and incessantly tapped her cigarette on the heavy glass ashtray in her lap. Chris sat in an armchair, hands clasped, watching Lane, who was at the fireplace. Lane poked the fire into crackling life, then selected and lifted a large log, heedless of damage to her clothes, and tossed it expertly, brushing herself as she watched the flames leap.

"More wine, Diana?" Lane asked.

"Thanks, no. I'm fine for now."

"What a pair of sissy drinkers," observed Liz, taking a deep swallow of bourbon. "How about a game of Scrabble? We'll draw for partners."

"I'll just fool around with my guitar," Millie said.

Lane said, "I'd like to look at your books."

Liz laughed, a harsh, sharp sound. "You know the only thing George wanted from the cabin? That collection of books over there, the matched set. Used to read them every time we came here. He loved those books. Begged me for them. I told him to go fuck himself."

They played Scrabble sitting on the floor around the coffee table, Diana and Madge partners against Liz and Chris. Diana had played frequently when she lived with Barbara, and she gave Liz a good match, enjoying the game, entertained by Liz's competitiveness. The contest remained close to the end, and Millie and Lane came over to watch, Lane kneeling beside Diana. Liz and Chris won by three points, and Liz shouted gleefully, "About damn time somebody gave me a good game! It's been a hell of a long time—since George, in fact."

Liz put the game away. "Better turn in, it'll be sunny tomorrow. Spring skiing, you've got to get out there early." She addressed Diana and Lane. "We have rules around here. We use the bathroom alphabetically by last name. That means you, Christianson."

With an amused smile, Lane obediently rose and left.

Liz watched until she disappeared through the doorway to the back of the cabin. "Very cool and uppity," she said to Madge.

"Give her time. She just needs to relax, Liz."

"She thinks she's better than any of us," Chris said.

"She sure doesn't have a thing to say to me," Millie said.

Madge shook her head. "I haven't been around Lane all that much, but I think she's just very tired."

"I like her," Diana stated, and in irritation walked over to the windows. "I've never been up here in the winter," she said. "Does the snow get very deep?"

"Sometimes it covers the cabin," Liz answered. "Drifts piled so high you have to shovel your way to the door. These are the elements, my dear." She was smiling at Diana's look of awe. "I think George loved that part of this place the most. What a shame," she said maliciously. "It's all mine now and he's not welcome, not even to visit. Kiss it goodbye, George—that's what I told him. No more cabin, George. As if I was about to let him screw his little floozy here when we had this place together for twenty years. I'd have burned it down first."

"Twenty years," Millie said. "You had this place the whole time you were married."

"Before. We came here on our honeymoon."

Lane, clad in blue silk pajamas, helped Diana draw the ladder up and lower the trapdoor. Then they stood in silver light and watched the winking lights of an aircraft drift across the glittering sky.

Lane said, "I remember skies like this up until I was ten, before we left Oklahoma."

"Dad used to take me camping in the mountains when I was small. We'd sit at night looking at the sky."

"I took beauty like this for granted when I was a child. Now I have to read poetry to recapture those feelings."

"What kind of poetry do you like?"

"I'm a hopeless romantic. Shelley, Keats, Dylan Thomas. Emily Dickinson is my favorite."

"Mine too." Diana shook her head, smiling. "We have odd things in common."

"Odd?"

"Unusual," Diana amended. "Surprising."

"I'm not surprised you like poetry."

"I grew up with it. Dad was forever quoting Kipling and Robert Burns."

"Your father sounds like quite a person."

"He is," Diana said with quiet pride. "He's a professor of English at Cal State Northridge and an absolutely marvelous father."

"That's nice to hear. I haven't read Robert Burns for years—but he's another romantic. My Emily Dickinson book, it's in about the same condition as my Peggy Lee record."

"I always read her selectively. When I read a lot of her at once she affects me too much. She's really a poet of grief, of loss."

"Yes. She truly is." In a voice so quiet Diana had to lean toward her to hear, Lane quoted,

"There is a pain — so utter —
It swallows substance up —
Then covers the Abyss with Trance —
So Memory can step
Around — across — upon it. . . ."

Silent with the thought of the agony that would cause Lane to commit such lines to memory, Diana stared bleakly at the snow.

"I don't mean to depress you," Lane murmured.

Diana said slowly, "Those words are powerful and terrible, even more so in all this snow, this cold." She continued thoughtfully, "Strange, of all her nature poems, I don't remember any about ice or snow or stars."

"She used this as a metaphor," Lane said, gesturing at the scene beyond the window. "For death, immortality. Her joy, her humor came out in her poems of summer."

"The ones I like best." She wondered if she should change this subject, which seemed so painful to Lane. She said tentatively, "I've seen Orion so many times but never in a setting like this."

"Where?"

"There, see? The rectangle with the three stars in it." Diana moved closer to Lane, sighting for her. There was the scent of perfume, delicate, elusive, pleasing. "See there?"

"Oh yes. It's beautiful."

"The brightest star in that corner is Rigel."

"Do you know astronomy? Other constellations?"

"Some of them."

"Will you show me?"

She slid an arm around Lane, feeling her warmth through the cool silk pajamas, and sighted again for her. "Over there, Cassiopeia, shaped like a W. Just follow the line from the Dipper handle straight through the North Star."

"Yes, I see it."

Diana continued to point out the constellations and major stars she knew. She said impulsively, "I've always had this dream of seeing the Southern Cross. It's simply four stars forming the shape of a cross. You can only see it in the southern hemisphere. I've imagined myself on a dark ocean on the deck of a ship looking at it, four jewels hanging in a warm black tropical sky."

Feeling foolish now, embarrassed, she said diffidently, "I guess mostly embezzlers go to South America. I doubt anyone's ever gone there just to look at the Southern Cross."

"Then you should be the first," Lane answered seriously. "People should do things like that. Know what I've always wanted to do? Run naked through the rain. I know that sounds adolescent—but I've always thought it would be such a feeling of exhilaration, even exultation."

"I think it would be wonderful."

After a moment Lane said, her voice warm with amusement, "We should go to South America together. You can drop me off on a nice warm tropical island where it's raining, and go on to contemplate your Southern Cross."

Chuckling, Diana gazed at the snow, thinking that Jack would have long since been bored; they would be making love by now. She asked, "Do the stars make you feel insignificant?"

"They're too remote," Lane answered. "Too many events on our own world make me feel insignificant enough." She moved away from Diana. "I guess we'd better get to bed. I'm glad it's warm up here. I didn't get a chance to get any flannel pajamas."

"I didn't bother. Flannel pajamas are awful. And who needs them in Southern California?"

They exclaimed over a huge down-filled quilt and pillows so soft that Diana, sighing luxuriously, piled three of them together.

"This is such a romantic room," Lane said. "I can understand why Liz won't sleep up here. It has to be where she spent her wedding night. And quite a few other nights, I'm sure."

"You're right. How insensitive of me not to realize that. It's not exactly designed for reading in bed, is it. Speaking of Liz, what was so funny about her books?"

"Oh God, you noticed. I did my best not to choke over those books. Promise you won't tell?" Lane's eyes glinted with merriment as she looked over at Diana from her pillows. "That set of so-called classics is actually a collection of pornography."

They laughed uproariously, and Diana gasped, "She doesn't know, does she."

"I'm sure not. She probably thought it was the cabin that brought out the romantic in her George."

They laughed again, and Diana said, "It's really sort of pitiful, Lane."

"Yes it is, Diana. I doubt she'll ever find out, though. The classics are the perfect place to hide pornography." Her voice brimmed with amusement. "Nobody ever reads them." She added in a sober tone, "I recommend you don't look. It's pretty sickening stuff."

"Okay." Diana settled herself on her pillows, pulled up the quilt. "How did you happen to go into law?"

"I followed my father. He communicated his love for the law so well I finally caught it myself."

"He must be very proud of you."

"I think he was. I hope he was. He died two years ago, a heart attack."

"I'm truly sorry," Diana said sincerely, remembering Lane's quiet voice reciting the Emily Dickinson poem.

"Thank you. I know you are, as close as you are to your father."

"Your work seems to take up a lot of your life." She had noticed that Lane wore a tiny gold watch and a chain bracelet, but no rings.

"I've managed to escape marriage, if that's what you mean. What about you?"

"I was married once, a long time ago. I can't imagine how you've managed to escape. Unless you don't believe in marriage. I don't. At least I don't think I do," she added.

"What do you object to? Making a commitment?"

"Least of all that. I don't like the ownership aspects."

"I see. I've had a close call or two, but . . . I sometimes think I should dye my hair. Blonde hair is such a symbol of a brainless, frivolous woman. I always seem to attract the wrong sort of men. Right now it's just as well, I work very long hours. It's very important to me to do well. Most of the men I work with think all women lawyers—I'm sorry, I didn't mean to make a speech. Should I continue droning on till I put you to sleep?"

Diana laughed. "You're very interesting."

"So are you. I enjoy talking to you."

Diana had formed another question to ask about her work, but Lane stretched tiredly and settled under the quilt. "Good night, Diana."

"Good night, Lane."

Diana lay waiting for sleep, drawing her thoughts away from the woman lying quietly next to her, but glad to have her there during this, her worst time of each night.

Again, as she did every night, she tested the armor of her icy, merciless rejection of Jack Gordon. And she remembered that every night for the past five years she had fallen asleep with Jack's body against hers; if they had made love she would lay her head on his chest, her arms around him, drowsily happy with her knowledge of his contentment, smelling his soap, his shaving cream, his cologne, and just faintly, the perspiration that had lightly, briefly coated his body when he had reached orgasm; and inhaling all the intoxicating scents of him, she would fall asleep instantly. The nights they did not make love she would fall asleep with her face pressed against the smooth muscle of his arm, her arm in the channel dividing his chest, her hand resting in the springy hair.

Remembering the feeling of the crisp curliness of Jack's hair under her fingers, she fell asleep.

Diana slept soundly, dreamlessly, and awakened to brilliant light. She sat up and stared, astounded. Unsuspected last night, the startling cobalt blue of Lake Tahoe glinted in the sun, surrounded by white mountains studded with dark feathery shapes of pine trees. Excitedly, she reached for Lane, and stopped, hand arrested.

Jack had looked helpless and endearing asleep, and she knew vulnerability was a quality often evident during sleep, but she was unprepared for the transformation of Lane Christianson. Rapt and fascinated, she stared at her, at the innocence of her face in repose, all of its alertness and intelligence shuttered away behind eyelids thickly fringed with gold eyelashes that lay softly on her cheeks. The tautness of her mouth was gone; her lips were tenderly shaped, sensual. She looked very young, and wistful, like a golden-haired child who had fallen asleep filled with hurt after a scolding.

"Lane," Diana said gently, not touching her.

Lane muttered in protest and rolled over, hiding her face with her hair and the folds of her pillow. Diana smiled and said again, "Lane." Lane stirred and Diana said softly, "Hey, wake up and look at the day."

Lane only reluctantly awakened, and sat up, looking at Diana sleepily. At Diana's gesture she glanced out the window, then stared. "Where on earth did that come from?"

"Somebody moved it in for us overnight." Diana quoted, " 'Beauty crowds me till I die.' "

"Wordsworth?"

"Our favorite poet."

"Our Emily said that?" Lane smiled, her sleepy eyes very blue against the backdrop of the sky, and ran her hands through her hair, brushing it back from her face.

"Yes. Our Emily."

Lane stretched lazily. "I think I can smell bacon through the floorboards. I hope."

"People who work long hours usually have terrible eating habits," Diana observed. "Is that how you stay so slender?"

"I eat enough for three people. I must be part hummingbird." She looked down at her body, frowning. "I'm all angles. You look like one of those soft pretty women they grow by the bushel down in Texas."

Pleased, Diana said, "I've heard that compliments from other women mean more because they're sincere."

"I think that's very true."

Diana's smile deepened. "As long as we're being sincere, I thought they only produced oil wells in Oklahoma, not such beautiful women."

Lane lowered her eyes. "Thank you," she murmured.

Astonished by her reaction, Diana said, "You've been told that a thousand times."

Lane continued to look away from her. "I wonder if Field Marshal Liz has us in alphabetical order again this morning. 'That means you, Christianson,' " she mimicked.

Diana chuckled, wondering at Lane's self-consciousness. Perhaps personal comments simply embarrassed her. But she seemed too poised, too self-possessed for that. She asked, "Are you going skiing?"

"Of course. Aren't you?" Lane was looking at her again, her arms crossed.

"No. I don't ski. I was thinking maybe you'd like to come into Tahoe with me, spend the day gambling."

"You don't ski? Not at all?"

"I tried it. Jack—a friend of mine took me up to Big Bear. All I did was fall down. And I knocked down a perfectly nice man who got up and brushed himself off and told me it was the first time he'd been on his feet for more than thirty seconds at a time and God must be sending him a message to quit. Well, that was it. I schussed and fell my way down the hill and hung up my poles forever."

Through her laughter Lane asked, "So you're a confirmed non-athlete?"

"I can get a tennis ball over the net. I like to walk. I used to break a hundred at golf."

"Used to? Did you hit someone on the golf course?"

Diana laughed; then she said thoughtfully, "Actually, it was a pleasant walk in nice surroundings, and other than that I don't think I ever did like it. What about gambling with me? Want to win some money?"

Lane hesitated. "I'd like to," she said finally. "But I'd better ski, I think."

"I guess that's healthier," Diana said, disappointed. She had felt certain that Lane would choose to go with her.

"I'm here as Madge's guest."

"Yes," Diana said, thinking it was a feeble reason.

"Maybe some strenuous exercise will help me relax. I need to."

"Yes. You do."

"So do you."

"You think so?" Diana asked, surprised.

"I could be wrong," Lane said. "I certainly don't know you very well, but you seem tense to me."

Diana smiled, and got out of bed. They donned robes and climbed down the ladder.

The women were drinking coffee around the fire. Liz said, "Sleep well, you two?"

"Yes," Diana said, breathing in the intoxicating aromas of coffee and bacon. "After we finally tore ourselves away from the window."

"Seen one star you've seen 'em all," Liz said with a shrug. "At least it's quiet up there. One weekend we had to pound on the ceiling with a broom handle to get some friends of Jerry's up."

"I'm a light sleeper," Diana said. "I could hear your voices this morning just faintly."

Lane said, "I sleep like a brick. Where's Chris?"

"In the bathroom, of course. It's alphabetical in reverse in the morning. To be fair. Holland, get in there," Liz said as Chris emerged. "That means you're last, Christianson. What's so damn funny?" she demanded.

"Nothing," Diana said, heading for the bathroom.

She dressed in a wine-colored wool sweater and pale gray pants.

Lane climbed down the ladder dressed in ski clothes, royal blue pants and sweater. The two women exchanged glances; Diana realized that they had quickly developed an awareness of each other, an affinity.

"Breakfast's ready," Liz called.

"Where do you want us to sit?" Lane asked with an impish grin at Diana as they went into the dining area.

"Roommates together, saves all that milling around. I must say you two are in a good mood this morning," Liz added as Diana and Lane laughed.

Diana took a second helping of scrambled eggs. "This mountain air really takes effect fast," she said.

"I hate people who can eat anything," Liz said. "You remind me of my oldest boy Jerry. Here, Lane, finish up this bacon."

After breakfast Liz announced, "Dishes are done in alphabetical order. Cook is exempt. Christianson and Dodd, go to it."

Diana sat on the hearth drinking coffee, interjecting an occasional comment into the conversation between Madge and Chris, as Liz marched about the cabin tidying and dusting. She watched Lane in the kitchen.

The white stripes across Lane's shoulders and down the arms of her sweater emphasized the slenderness and straightness of her body. Ski pants, stretched tautly over her legs, outlined the slim curve of hip, the long lines of her thighs and legs. She dried and put dishes away, stretching and reaching to the shelves, blonde hair changing patterns as she moved, her body supple and graceful, and Diana watched her with pleasure, enjoying her beauty.

The women left in a flurry of activity and an accumulation of ski equipment. As she locked the cabin door, Liz said to Diana, "Dinner at seven. That any problem?"

"Not at all. I'll look forward to it."

"Madge says she has something a little different planned for tonight. Says we'll find it very interesting."

Diana drove slowly down Highway 50 toward Stateline and the casinos, remembering when she had discovered this place — the three brilliant exhilarating summer days here with Barbara, when they had shared the grandeur of the Sierras and the shimmering beauty of Lake Tahoe along with the excitement of gambling.

She looked around her with keen interest; it had been four years since her last visit. She had stayed in a lakefront condominium with Jack in the late spring, reveling in the crisp freshness of the air, the traces of snow on the rugged tree-laden mountains surrounding the Lake, the deep cold harmonies of blue in the water just outside their window. She had not realized that Jack had been bored until he demurred when she wanted to return.

"Vegas is closer," he had said, "and more fun."

She came to the brief stretch along Highway 50 that skirted the shoreline; and she looked through the trees, braking the car slightly to savor the view across the vivid patterns of blue to the mountains. She sped up with an apologetic wave as the car behind her honked its irritation.

She walked into Harrah's smiling at the familiar rush of casino noise that engulfed her, the whir and ring of slot machines, the unremitting buzz of gambling activity. She searched for Vivian.

This early, Harrah's was not crowded; sections of the club were deserted, leather covers on the blackjack tables. Three sections were open, only a few of the tables crowded with gamblers. Diana strolled through a cluster of blackjack tables, scanning the black-and-white clad dealers—the men neat in their white shirts and black ties, the women wearing white blouses, all the dealers wearing nametags and black aprons with *Harrah's* stenciled in gold. They stood in various attitudes of disinterest, some dealing the cards with cool dispassion, some talking to their tables of patrons, others standing with arms crossed—no one at their tables—looking vaguely out over the crowd circulating unceasingly through the casino. By contrast, the dealers at the craps tables were in continual motion, leaning to collect and pay off bets, swiftly stacking chips between rolls of the dice. Two dealers at an empty craps table talked to each other, one of them desultorily stacking, destroying, restacking a column of black hundred-dollar chips.

Diana paused at a roulette table. Six players were covering the layout liberally with bright chips of varying colors. The dealer pulled in mounds of chips with each settling of the ball, piling them into stacks of equal height and color with incredible rapidity. Diana enjoyed the spectacle of the game with no wish to play; she had no feel for numbers and only a basic understanding of the game. One man at the table was winning steadily, accumulating large stacks of purple chips with each settling of the roulette ball. He was tall, sandy-haired, good-looking. He reminded her of Jack. Pain began, and she closed her eyes against it in weary resentment. She spotted Vivian.

Vivian hugged her, and Diana said affectionately, "I bet you've been gambling to beat hell already."

"Late night," murmured Vivian. Her eyes were puffy, her face pale.

"Did you have breakfast?"

Vivian nodded. "We had room service before John left for his sales seminar. It's good to have you here, Diana dear. How are things at the cabin? If it's a real bore Vivian will get you out of there. Liz and I have a very honest relationship."

"I'll only see them in the evening. And no hotel could possibly be as beautiful. The setting—"

"I thought you'd like it. I spent two weeks with George and Liz and their two boys years ago. I lost a hundred dollars I couldn't afford, but it was the most beautiful time I ever spent anywhere." Vivian added simply, "I thought it would be good for you."

"It's great. Let's play blackjack, tiger."

"Just for a little while, to keep you company. Vivian isn't as good at that game as you are, honey."

"Only because Vivian bets hunches. That's not the way to give yourself a chance to win."

"Vivian is unlucky, that's all."

They sat at a blackjack table, and Diana changed a twenty-dollar bill. She brushed the green felt of the table with her fingertips and hefted a stack of chips enjoyably, with a sense of well-being and excitement. For the first time in years, she was on a gambling trip that had nothing to do with Jack. She was here on her own, because she wanted to be here.

"I'm playing a hunch," she told Vivian, and made a ten dollar bet. Her two cards were the ace and jack of spades.

"I don't believe it," she said.

"Let's hear it for hunches." Vivian grinned triumphantly. "You should've bet everything you have."

She returned to the cabin just before seven. The women had changed from their snow gear into what seemed to be standard cabin attire: Madge and Millie in blue and grey sweatsuits, Chris and Liz wearing heavy knit sweaters and jeans that bagged out over their ample hips.

"Where's Lane?" she asked Madge.

Madge shrugged. "In the shower. All that snow made her dirty."

"I see you haven't pawned your car yet," Liz called. She stabbed at steaks on a portable grill.

Diana strolled into the kitchen. "As a matter of fact, I'm about fifty dollars ahead."

"What do you play?" asked Chris. She was preparing a salad.

"Don't encourage Chris, she's already lost her shirt," Liz growled.

"Blackjack," Diana answered Chris. "But I must confess I won most of it dropping a quarter in a slot machine. I was waiting for Viv to give up so we could get some lunch."

"I work for hours and you drop a quarter in," Chris said.

"Exactly what Viv yelled."

"How's Viv doing?" Liz inquired, her dark eyes amused.

"Losing, I'm afraid."

"She'll leave here screwed every which way."

"Liz," Chris said disapprovingly.

"Hi." Lane came into the kitchen buttoning the sleeves of a pale yellow corduroy shirt tucked into dark brown jean-style pants. Her skin glowed with heightened color; the ends of her hair were a slightly darker blonde with dampness from the shower. "So how was your day?"

"Good," Diana said, looking at her with pleasure. "How about you?"

Chatting, they took glasses of wine over to the fire. "I did pretty well skiing," Lane said. "I was pleased."

Millie said, "She did fantastic."

"Meaning I managed to stay upright some of the time," Lane said with a grin. "It's been a long time. I was going on instinct. Tomorrow I'll think about what I'm doing and spend the day falling on my head."

Diana enjoyed her dinner, listening peacefully to talk of ski slopes and conditions, ski resorts, ski clothes, ski equipment. After dinner she and Chris did the dishes. Liz and Madge sat around the fire drinking coffee and playing Yahtzee; Lane, curled up in an armchair, read a paperback.

"Okay everybody," Madge said. "We're going to play some encounter games."

"Oh for God's sake, Madge," Millie said. "That went out in the sixties."

"The hell it did," Madge retorted. "Maybe as a fad, yes. The nudist groups, people like that, maybe. But it's a common psychological tool now. All kinds of people form T groups. People who want a self-actualizing experience. Fat people, child abusers—even compulsive gamblers." Madge smiled with sardonic friendliness at Diana.

Liz said, "We came up here to have fun, not bare our souls."

"We won't get into anything like that at all. This *is* fun, a technique for being more open, seeing how other people see you. We have a good group here, a blend of people who know each other and some who don't, to sort of validate the process."

"Well, it sounds kind of interesting," Millie said doubtfully.

"Exactly what do we do?" Chris asked, her eyes wide with anxiety.

"Play a series of little games. We'll need to form into a circle first. I'll explain things as we go along. Liz, where do you think everybody should sit?"

Diana exchanged an amused glance with Lane over this transparent manipulation of Liz.

But Liz scowled. "Do we really want to do this? Who wants to?"

"Sounds sort of interesting," Millie said with a shrug. "Okay by me."

"I'll try it for a while," Chris said grudgingly.

"Okay with me," Diana said.

"Me too," Lane said.

"Let's get something to drink first," Liz said. "Loosen all of us up."

Diana poured wine for herself and Lane, and when the women returned with their drinks Madge said, "Now let's sit on the floor by the fire, in a cozy circle."

"Millie, you sit beside me," Liz ordered. "Lane on the other side of me—or maybe Diana. No, I think Lane, but Diana next to Lane. Then Madge. No, Chris. Then Madge."

The women laughed and pushed at each other as they milled around following Liz's conflicting instructions.

Liz bellowed, "Sit down, dammit!"

Madge said, as the group assembled in a loose circle before the fire, "We'll use Liz as the top of our circle to get the partnerships straight. First, you shake hands with the person to the right and left of you."

"These games better pick up damn fast," Liz said. "God, is this dumb. Nothing personal," she added to Lane, turning to her with hand outstretched.

Diana shook Chris's dry, rough hand, and then turned to Lane. Lane's slim cool hand took hers firmly.

"Hi," Lane said with a grin. " 'I'm Nobody! Who are you?' "

Diana laughed delightedly. " 'Then there's a pair of us?' "

"What's all this nonsense?" Liz demanded, dark eyes alert, curious.

"Just something a reclusive lady named Emily said one time." Lane smiled mischievously at Diana.

Madge said, "Come on, everybody. Now hold hands with the person to your right, and look into her eyes for a full minute without speaking. I'll time you. Then somebody can time me."

"At least I'll have something pretty to look at," Liz said, turning to Lane, taking her hands. "You'll have to settle for my old sourpuss."

"With pleasure," Lane said easily.

Diana took Chris's hands.

"Everybody ready? One minute. Go."

Fingers fluttered in Diana's hands. Pale blue eyes stared into hers with an uncertainty that grew with each passing second. Diana looked into Chris's eyes with increasing sympathy, and smiled reassuringly. Chris smiled back, her eyes shy and softening perceptibly. Their gazes were warm, their hands gripping tightly, when Madge said, "Time."

Wonderingly assessing the small miracle between herself and Chris, Diana watched Madge look into Millie's eyes as Liz timed them. Lane, looking off into the fire, seemed bemused by her experience with Liz.

"Time," Liz called; and Diana reached for Lane's hands, warming them in hers.

"Begin," said Madge.

First Diana saw gray-blue color, then growing awareness—then tenderness. Lane's eyes widened, closed, slowly opened again. Diana gazed at her longing to surround the tenderness with warmth, wanting to hold it enclosed and protected, wishing she could hold her face in her hands. Her hands tightened; she tried to convey her feeling with pressure from her fingers, certain she could not express it with only her eyes.

"Time," called Madge; and Diana discovered that she and Lane had swayed toward each other. Diana loosened her grip; Lane continued to hold her hands for seconds longer.

Still absorbed in the emotion of her experience with Lane, Diana watched the slow softening of expression as Madge and Chris looked into each other's eyes.

"That was wonderful," Chris murmured as Liz called time. There were other murmurs of agreement.

"It shows how people don't really look at each other," Madge said. "Now we touch. Turn to the person on your right and close your eyes and touch her face with your hands, your fingers, any way you'd like to. For a minute. The two of you decide who touches first."

Diana turned to Chris and suggested softly, "Why don't you touch me first, Chris?"

"Begin," Madge said; and Chris, eyes closed tightly, touched Diana's face with gentle, tremulous fingers. At the end of the minute, Diana stroked the soft dry skin of Chris's face; and afterward the two women smiled warmly.

Diana turned to Lane. She said from a wellspring of emotion, "I'd like to touch you first."

"Begin," Madge said.

Diana closed her eyes and reached to Lane. Warm hands took hers and led them. Diana traced the shape of Lane's face, drawing fingertips across her forehead and slowly down over her cheekbones, pleased by tactile sensations of soft smooth warm sculpture. But her mind was flooded by images of Lane's sleeping face and Lane's eyes gazing into hers filled with helpless tenderness, and Diana cupped her face gently, fingertips caressing her temples, until Madge said, "Time."

Then Lane's slender fingers touched Diana's face, moving for a moment into her hair, then very slowly down over her forehead, tracing her eyebrows; and then very gently over her eyelids, down her cheeks and lightly across Diana's lips, fingertips resting in the corners. Diana sat unmoving, transfixed, overwhelmed by the tenderness of her touch and the still beauty of her face.

"Time."

Lane's eyes opened; they seemed gray and unfocused; and she blinked rapidly as if waking from sleep. Then she looked at Diana. Their eyes met for a single moment so intensely connecting that Diana felt it as a caress. She looked away, astonished by her feeling; and as she watched Millie stroke Madge's face, she wondered if she could have imagined the moment.

"I can see why encounter was so popular," Millie said afterward, squeezing Madge's hands.

"It can be a peak experience," Madge said, beaming at Millie. "Some of the people I met at my first encounter group went on to other groups, and I did too. Trying to recapture the feeling. Some people went to a lot of them. Like junkies for the experience."

"I need another drink after all this closeness," Liz said, rising stiffly to her feet. "I need to be well lubricated if I'm going to have these old bones on the floor."

"How about more wine?" Lane asked Diana.

"I'll come with you."

"Don't insulate yourselves with liquor," Madge cautioned. "Just be relaxed. Too much booze can bring out negatives and distort what's really trying to happen."

Liz poured a generous quantity of bourbon over ice and returned to the living room. With an emotion she could not identify, Diana asked in a low tone, "What was it like looking at Liz?"

Lane refilled their wine glasses, her lips curving into a cold smile. "Two gunfighters in Dodge City at high noon."

Diana chuckled. "I'd just let her shoot me."

"Not me." Lane's tone was flat, hard.

Diana continued to glance at her when they returned to the circle by the fire, assimilating the steeliness she had discovered in Lane Christianson. She could now visualize her in a courtroom: cool, precise, competent.

"What's next, maestro?" Liz said, raising her glass.

Madge extinguished a half-smoked cigarette, lit another. "A trust game. We prove that we're capable and worthy of trust. This is a physical game, so let's stand up and get together by size."

Diana, an inch or two shorter than Lane, stood beside her. Liz promptly moved beside her sister. Millie took her place beside Madge.

Madge said, "You stand with your back to your partner, about three feet in front of her, and fall backwards. You trust her to catch you."

"Oh come on," Millie said, and went over to the coffee table to get her drink. "That's as easy as pie, Madge."

"You'll be surprised," Madge said. She inhaled deeply from her fresh cigarette. "It's very difficult to do. It's very hard for most people to trust other people."

"That depends who it is," Chris said. "I trust Liz."

"Then why don't you go first?"

"Me?" Chris looked at Madge with mild reproach. "Well, all right." She took her place in front of Liz. Shifting her feet uneasily, she peered over her shoulder.

"No looking," instructed Madge. "This is trust."

"Okay, I'm ready now." But she hesitated, feet shuffling nervously.

"Come on, Chris," Liz coaxed. "If you can't trust me, who can you trust?" She held out her arms.

"It's very hard for most people to do this," Madge said. "You'll see when you try it."

"I'm ready now." Squeezing her eyes shut, Chris swayed backward, then caught herself.

"I'm right here for you, Chris. Right here."

Her face stiff with fear, Chris fell backward and Liz caught her with a merry "Whoops!" as the women laughed and applauded.

"How was it?" Madge asked, stubbing out her cigarette. She shook another out of her pack.

Smiling with relief, her voice tremulous, Chris said, "It was hard. It was kind of like jumping out of a hayloft when Liz and I were kids."

"Your turn now, Liz," Madge said. "Trust Chris."

Liz took her place in front of Chris, planting her feet firmly. Her face and body rigid with tension, she fell into Chris's arms.

"You do trust me, don't you Liz?" Chris asked softly.

"I don't mind telling you I was a little nervous," Liz said. "Being heavier than you." She touched a hand to her sister's face. "Yes, I trust you, Chrissie." She looked challengingly at Lane. "How about you next, hotshot? I bet it takes a lot to scare you."

"This isn't a test of courage," Madge interjected firmly. "Only of trust." She lit another cigarette; Diana thought she saw her hands tremble.

Lane stood in front of her. "Ready back there?"

"Ready," Diana said, braced and waiting for her.

"Sure you even want to catch me?" Lane joked as she hesitated.

"Maybe, maybe not," Diana teased.

"Sure you even want to try it, hotshot?" Liz taunted.

Diana saw Lane's shoulders tense, her hands clench; then she fell back and Diana caught her easily. Smiling down at her, she held Lane's slender body for a moment, the corduroy of her shirt warm and soft in her hands, then dropped her with a thump to the floor. "That's for not trusting me."

Lane lay on the floor laughing; the women laughed uproariously. Diana, smiling, held out her hands and helped Lane up.

Lane took her place behind Diana. "Now it's my turn to catch you." She added a mock-threatening chuckle. "And that'll take real courage. Think you can trust me?"

"Yes," Diana said with utter certainty, and let her body fall into Lane's arms. She smiled up at her. "Remember, revenge is not nice."

"You trusted me so much I almost wasn't ready for you," Lane said gently, helping her to her feet.

Millie fell trustingly into Madge's arms, and Madge took her place in front of Millie. Taking deep drags from her cigarette, she made many attempts, teetering back and forth, her eyes closed, her thin body rigid. The women cajoled, teased, taunted, encouraged.

"I can't do it," she said finally. "I just can't, goddammit. I can never do this one. I've tried and tried."

"How about I stand behind you," Liz said. "I'm big and strong enough to catch King Kong."

"It isn't that," Madge said, sighing. "I just can't do it. Let's go on to something else." She extinguished her cigarette in a smoldering mound of butts and ashes.

The group assembled again in a circle around the fire. Madge said, "What we'll do now is decide which animal each of us represents."

Liz snorted and picked up her bourbon. Millie looked bewildered.

"Think about it," Madge said. "Each of us will remind you of some animal, if you really think about it. Let's do me first. What animal do I make you think of?"

The women were quiet and reflective, scrutinizing Madge. Lane said slowly, "I think maybe a giraffe." She continued as Liz laughed, "To me they seem always to be searching, to be curious about everything, always looking around to see new things."

Madge nodded, her expression rueful. "One group I was in said giraffe too. The other said flamingo."

"Flamingo is very good," Liz said thoughtfully, studying Madge.

Madge fidgeted under Liz's gaze. "Let's do you next, Liz."

"I think Liz is a bear," Chris said. "Strong and self-sufficient. I know if anybody ever hurt her boys she'd go after them just like a bear with cubs."

Liz sipped her bourbon, then said in a level tone, "I would kill. My boys are everything. Especially now."

"Bear is good," Lane said. "I think elephant, too. For most of the same reasons. Strength, dominance, the need to control a domain."

"Why can't someone choose an animal that doesn't reflect on my weight?" Liz complained good-naturedly.

Madge said, "Lane, you seem to have natural insight for this. Let's do Diana now."

Prickling with self-consciousness, Diana looked at the floor as the women contemplated her.

"I think she's a doe," Chris said. "She has a sweetness and a gentleness to her."

"Yes, but without the helplessness," Madge said. "Maybe a deer instead of a doe."

"I think a cat," Millie said in her soft shy voice. "That's a sweet gentle animal."

"Close, but not quite right," Liz said. "I see Chris as a cat."

"A jungle cat seems more like it for Diana," Lane said. "The feminine qualities combine with strength."

"I saw a jaguar on *Wild Kingdom* not too long ago," Chris said. "They're simply lovely."

"Jaguar is good," Lane said.

"I agree with Liz that Chris is a cat," Madge said.

"I do too," Diana said, relieved to have their attention diverted from her.

"A nice tabby cat I hope," Chris said.

"Sure, why not?" Liz smiled at her sister. "What about Lane? What's her animal?"

"An eagle," Diana said immediately.

"What an unusual choice!" Chris exclaimed.

Millie flung out her arms. "Eagles are lovely birds, so strong, so noble."

"They're independent and free," Diana said testily, irritated by Millie's theatrics.

"And lonely," Madge added. "Lonely up there in their rocks looking out over the world."

"You make me seem terribly romantic," Lane said.

"Eagles have talons," Liz said sharply. "They swoop down and take what they want."

"No longer so romantic," Lane said with an easy smile at Liz.

"Let's do Millie," Diana suggested, irked now with Liz.

"I think Millie's a doe. No, a deer," Madge said.

"She definitely has a vulnerable quality," Lane said.

"I think deer too," Liz said. "The elephant wants to get on with another game. What's next, Madge?"

"Let's choose a one word description that best sums up and describes each other. Let's begin with uh, Lane. We'll move to her right, each one of us in turn. What do you think of Lane overall in one word, Diana?"

After a moment of concentrated thought, Diana said, "Gentle and sensitive."

"Hmmph," Liz said, picking up her drink.

"One word," Madge said to Diana.

"It's hard to choose. I guess . . . sensitive. It suggests gentle."

"I don't see that at all," Liz challenged, her dark eyes fixed on Lane.

Diana said icily. "Well, it's my—"

"We'll hear your opinion in a minute, Liz," Madge said placatingly. "Chris?"

"I'm trying to think of a word that means hard to figure out or get close to," Chris mused. "Distant? Mysterious? I guess mysterious."

"Much more like it," Liz said, nodding and crossing her arms.

Madge cast a reproving glance at Liz. "My turn." She looked at Lane for some moments, reflecting. "Something in your script is driving you, but I think I'll choose dedicated for my word."

Lane smiled at her. "Dedicated sounds much better than driven."

Madge said with quiet emphasis, "Still, you *are* driven."

Millie whispered, "I think I'd choose remote to describe Lane." She sat cross-legged, eyes fixed on her hand as it picked at the material of her sweatsuit.

"And I'll say cool," Liz said. "You see, Diana? You see a very different person than the rest of us."

Diana swallowed a sharp retort, unwilling to pursue this discussion, filled with distaste at the prospect of debating Lane with Liz or any of the women. She said instead, firmly, "I see what I see."

"I feel like the subject of a soap commercial," Lane said, her voice expressionless.

Madge said, "For what it's worth, except for Diana, we've described you pretty much as a person who's . . . detached."

Lane leaned back casually, legs stretched out, hands on the carpet behind her to brace herself. She smiled at the women. "I'll have to work on bringing Diana's dissenting opinion into line with the rest of yours."

"Cool. Very cool," Liz said, raising her glass in a toast.

Madge stared at Liz. "Diana's next. Give us a one word description, Chris."

"That's so easy. Sweet. Diana's sweet."

Madge mused, gazing at Diana, "She is sweet, Chris, in a nice old-fashioned sort of way. The kind of woman men like to marry. Pretty, a good figure. A girl just like the girl that married dear old dad. I'll say nice."

Startled, disconcerted, awkward under the appraising eyes of the group, Diana laughed nervously.

"I'll say sweet," Millie said. "I like Chris's word."

"I'd agree with nice," Liz said, "but to me nice people are boring, and she's not boring." She looked at Diana reflectively, through narrowed eyes. "I don't know her very well, but from what I've heard and seen, I'd say honest. I pick up a strong feeling of honesty from her."

"I agree with all your words, especially honest," Lane said. She sat with one leg drawn up, a hand dangling over the knee, gazing into the fire. "The word I would choose would be . . . warm."

"Diana, you certainly make a good impression," Madge said, her eyebrows raised.

"I'm just lucky none of you know me very well," Diana murmured, flushed with embarrassment.

She listened with only part of her mind as the game continued. She had already chosen shy as her word for Chris, would describe Madge as searching, Millie as unaffected, Liz as strong. She watched Lane, turning over in her mind the disparity between the women's view and her own. Certain of her reading of Lane as a warm and complex woman, she was curious but undisturbed; Lane had arrived at the cabin only two hours before her—not much time for the formation of a more considered opinion by the others. But she was puzzled by Lane's seeming lack of concern for their judgment. An extension of a demeanor adopted for professional reasons? A mask for aspects of herself she thought might be interpreted as weakness—a deliberately constructed defense? Yet she had revealed herself to Diana from their first meeting before the fire. That could not have been accidental. Perhaps she felt safe with a woman who would soon return to Los Angeles, who she would probably never see again.

"What's next up your sleeve, Madge?" Liz asked.

"Some strokes. Let's start with you and move to your left. Tell the group what you like about Millie."

"Her generosity," Liz said readily, and took a long swallow of bourbon. "Millie can be a pain, but she'd give you the shirt off her back."

Millie beamed.

"Toss in her bra too, if you're a man."

"Your turn, Millie," Madge said as Millie stared at Liz, her smile fading. "Is there anything at all about me that you like?"

Millie sighed, looked at Madge. "Sure. Lots of things. You're so interested in new ideas, and you're entertaining. You have a dry sense of humor I like."

"Liz is right, you're a generous person," Madge said. "What I like about Chris is her good heart. She's a kind person, and it's her basic nature."

"Oh what a lovely thing to say, Madge!" Chris turned to Diana and said falteringly, "She's such a lovely girl, that's what I like about Diana. So sweet and gentle, someone I'd like to have for a daughter."

Diana, very moved, looked at Chris, moisture coming to her eyes. Chris was no older than her mid-forties, yet the lonely old woman in her was already visible. Diana took Chris's hand and squeezed it.

She cleared her throat and looked at Lane. "What I like about Lane is her appreciation of her life, and that she wants her life to have meaning."

"Very high sounding sentiments," Liz said. "What does it mean?" She drained the rest of her bourbon.

"Thank you," Lane said to Diana. "What I like about Liz is her strength and confidence. They're such rare qualities. Most people are too insecure to really express themselves as individuals."

Surely this belligerent woman would be disarmed by such a compliment, Diana thought.

"Except you and me, right babe?" Liz sneered.

Lane did not reply. Diana was mystified by Liz's hostility.

"Anybody besides me want more to drink?" Liz got to her feet with difficulty. "My ass is falling asleep. Somebody toss a log on the fire."

Liz and Chris went to the kitchen, Madge and Millie to the bathroom.

"Like more wine?" Diana asked as Lane selected a log.

"No, I've got plenty, thanks."

"What's with her?" Diana inclined her head toward the kitchen.

Lane threw the log on the fire and straightened it with a thrust of the poker. "Bourbon, probably. Don't worry about it."

"Anybody want grass?" Madge was rummaging through her purse.

"You've got grass?" Liz had returned from the kitchen. "What the hell were you saving it for?"

"I don't have much. We're going to be here all week."

"Tell me," Liz demanded, sitting down and peering at Lane, "what does our lady barrister have to say about grass?"

"Simple possession of marijuana is a misdemeanor in the state of California."

"Does that mean we go to the gas chamber?"

Lane smiled. "Only if you kill somebody while you're smoking it."

Madge lit a joint and passed it to Chris. To Diana's surprise, Chris took a deep drag and passed it to her, explaining apologetically, "Everybody I know in San Francisco smokes. I finally tried it and I must confess I like it better than alcohol."

Diana passed the joint to Lane, who gave it to Liz. Liz said sweetly, "You girls don't indulge?"

"It makes me stupid and sleepy," Diana said.

"I like wine," Lane said.

Liz took a long drag, inhaled deeply. "If you ask me, our dear little barrister doesn't want to be a lawbreaker, that's all. She doesn't smoke, drink, or swear, if you notice. But you're not too pure to fuck, are you dear."

"No," Lane said calmly.

"And fuck a lot, too. Really fuck up a storm."

"Liz, stop that," Chris said. "You're being nasty. Perfectly nasty, and for no reason."

Liz grinned at her sister. "Far be it from me to be nasty to dear Lane. As in Mar-lane-a," she continued, drawing out the name, "namesake of another, much older blonde bombshell. What's next, Madge sweetie?"

Madge was looking cautiously from Lane to Liz. "Well, we repay the strokes we've just received with a negative. You talk about the person who just said something nice about you, you mention something about her you'd like to see her change, something you think is a negative. We'll discuss it as a group, whether we agree or disagree."

"This should be very interesting," Liz said, crossing her arms.

"Let's start with uh, Diana."

"Well," Diana said carefully, as Chris's pale blue eyes searched hers anxiously, "I'd like to see Chris have greater tolerance for other people . . . more understanding about . . . life experiences that make people . . . different from her and what she knows."

"I agree with that completely," Madge said, inhaling deeply and passing a joint to Millie. "And very well said, too. Everyone lives by their own script, we should all work at understanding that."

Millie inhaled and said, "People should have more faith and belief in other people."

"Bullshit," Liz said, waving away the offer of the joint and picking up her bourbon. "And I'm not just coming to the defense of my sister, either. For chrissake, you goddam bleeding hearts. Where does understanding leave off and judgment begin? You certainly could use a little judgment, Millie. You believe in other people and all they ever do is fuck you. Front and back, and especially in the ass."

"Liz!" Chris protested.

"Some people aren't worthy of trust," Millie said with dignity. "Some people just take what they want and throw everything else away like a banana peel. That's their sin, not mine."

"You're being intolerant," Liz said smugly.

"You can be judgmental without condemning," Diana said with irritation, "that's all I meant. You have to make judgments about people all the time, but they shouldn't be so rigid and your mind so closed that you can't consider adjusting your opinions as you learn and grow."

"That's not adjusting, that's compromising. Compromising your principles."

"Hardly," Diana said caustically.

"Times have changed so," Chris said thickly, "it's so hard to keep up. People talk about things—people *do* things we didn't even whisper about when we were growing up."

Madge said, "You're just following your own bad script, Chris. You're not able to break away from it even when you want to. You and Liz." She lit another joint.

"Bullshit." Liz took another deep swallow from her drink. "You and your fucking scripts. I do what I damn please, not what some crackpot psychiatrist says I'm programmed to do. That's garbage. That's bullshit."

"Liz," Chris said, "please." She continued in a pleading voice, "Madge—Liz and I couldn't be more different. We were brought up so strictly, you know. Mother always said we should demand the best in our lives, not settle for anything less. She gave us high standards to live by. But Liz went one way and I went another."

"You can interpret script instructions differently." Madge pulled at her hair with tense, nicotine-stained fingers. "It's still a script."

Liz glared at Madge, who drew again on a joint passed from Millie. Diana asked Chris gently, "Is there some reason you didn't marry? You'd have made a wonderful mother."

"I love children," Chris whispered. "There just was . . . never anyone quite right. There were lots of chances but nothing . . . that was quite the best . . . quite right."

"The never-good-enough script," Madge said, nodding. "Scripty behavior. Scripty language."

"Fucking bullshit," Liz snarled.

"Well, I think there's something in what Diana says," Chris said. "Maybe I have been too unbending. But it's too late to really change things now."

Lane had been sitting quietly, sipping wine. She said, "No it's not, Chris. Not if you want to badly enough."

"That's easy for you to say," Liz said. "How old are you?"

"Thirty-two."

"I'm forty-three and Chris is forty-five. We don't have a face and body like yours to put on display. If I had your body I wouldn't be giving it away and I wouldn't be any damn lawyer either." Gently, Liz took a butt which had burned down to Chris's fingers, and crushed it in the ashtray. "Shit, I'd be in business for myself. A hundred bucks a night comes out to thirty-six thousand five hundred a year. Plus bonuses."

The women, including Lane, laughed in escalating peals.

"Of course," Liz said, staring at Lane, "I like fucking a lot, too."

Lane stared back at her. "Good for you."

"Cool," Liz said, smiling at her. "Very, very cool."

Lane turned to Chris. "Thirty-two isn't young—but it's true you and Liz have more life experience than I. You can still make major decisions about your life up to the point of senility. People do that. There are all kinds of examples."

"All I ever wanted to do was fuck my husband," Liz said.

"Liz was always so sure of what she wanted," Chris said, staring off toward the fire. "So blunt, so sure, so earthy about her needs. I was always more romantic. You know, I never even found a man who wanted to kiss me enough without, you know, wanting to do the other immediately. Men just don't know things. What women want. Like how much we like to kiss."

"Some women," Liz said. "Not me. It's not the pale moon that excites *me*."

"A lot of women," Lane said. "This woman. But not all men are like that, Chris. Some of them can't be bothered finding out, but not all of them."

Liz glared, and Diana said hastily, impelled to defend Chris and Lane, "This woman too."

"I couldn't agree more," Millie said. "Kissing is lovely. I think you can tell someone everything you think and feel with a kiss."

Lane quoted softly,

> *"We talked with each other about each other*
> *Though neither of us spoke . . ."*

"Written by a deaf-mute," Liz said scornfully.

The women laughed at Liz, except for Millie who lit a fresh joint and said unhappily, "Really, you can never tell what kind of a clod you're going to find in bed. God, some of them are so crude."

"True," Lane said. "Too true."

Millie continued in an aggrieved tone, "They think we're nothing but two breasts and a vagina."

Madge said, "Vaginas are out. Clitorises are in."

"The hell you say," Liz said. "My favorite song is "Great Balls of Fire." Just give me a good hard hot cock."

"You see what I mean?" Chris said to Diana. "People talk about just incredible things today."

"Some men don't even know what a clitoris is," Millie complained, "let alone where it is."

"I should hang a sign on mine," Madge said. "Do not fold,

spindle or mutilate. Arthur pushes on mine like he's ringing a doorbell. Arthur is my husband," she explained to Diana, who was laughing helplessly.

"Why don't you tell the dumb son of a bitch?" Liz said indifferently. She sipped her bourbon and took a quick puff from Millie's joint.

"You know better than that. Tell a man anything about sex and it's like stepping on a scorpion. And I have told him. Told him and told him. He still does it. I leap in the air with pain and he thinks it's sexual frenzy."

Chris said, ignoring the laughter of the women, "I think you live very dangerously, Millie. That singles bar of yours, you just take a terrible chance."

"That's silly, Chris. We're not all looking for Mr. Goodbar." Millie pushed at the blonde frizz around her face. "I used to think Mom and Daddy were funny because they always went to this beer bar all the time, but now I understand. They had friends there they cared about. Singles bars aren't the awful places they're made out to be. They're like . . . clubs. You get to know people, you even care about some of them. Where it ends is up to you, just like anywhere else." Her soft voice trailed off. "You can find sex anywhere . . ."

Madge said, "It's in your script. Your parents went to a place like that and you think they've given you orders to do the same."

"Jesus Christ," Liz said, rolling her eyes upward. "Scripts. I need another drink." She climbed to her feet. "Scripts scripts scripts," she muttered, marching to the kitchen.

"It's just not good to drift from one affair to another, Millie," Chris said. "How would you know if the real thing came along?"

Lane said, "People often confuse the real thing with something that should have been an affair."

"Lane's right." Millie nodded eagerly. "Look at all the divorces."

"People should be able to handle butterfly interludes," Lane said, smiling at Millie.

"But so many?" Chris said doubtfully.

"Butterfly interludes are very different from the real thing," Lane said.

"But butterfly interludes are so superficial," Diana said, disliking the term.

"They're meant to be," Lane said. "They shouldn't be given any deeper significance."

"Let's go on," Madge said. "It's your turn, Chris. What would you like to see me change?"

"Well . . . nothing really. Well, maybe . . . it's hard to get a real grip on you, that's all. You've got opinions and ideas and lots of enthusiasm about what interests you, but I'm not sure I know who the real Madge is. Does that make any sense?"

Madge took a final puff from the tiny end of a joint and crushed it. She lit another as no one spoke. "Anybody agree with that? Did you hear, Liz?"

Liz took her place in the circle holding a tumblerful of bourbon in which a single ice cube floated. "I heard. And yes, since you ask. There are times I'd like to shake you till your teeth rattle and the real Madge comes out." She swallowed some bourbon. "You jump from one crackpot idea to another and every time you say this one's the right one, this one's eternal truth. Then a week or a month later you've gone on to the next eternal truth."

"I think every time it might be," Madge said in a low voice. She stared at the floor. "There might be . . . answers."

Diana gazed at her, stricken with pity.

"There's a lot to you, I'm sure," Millie said, "but sometimes you remind me of those terribly superficial women from Southern California. No offense," she added to Diana.

"We have them," Diana said, thinking tartly that this woman had little room to talk, this Northern California woman who drifted from one liaison to another.

Madge said, "I can't change my—" She saw the expression on Liz's face and amended her words, "I'm not sure how . . . I don't know how to change."

"Live your life instead of observing and analyzing it all the time." Abruptly, Liz asked, "Where's Arthur tonight?"

Madge blinked in surprise. "I suppose home or playing cards with his friends."

"Why did he let you come up here for a week by yourself?"

"Liz," Madge said, pulling at her hair, "Liz, you know very well we allow each other room to breathe."

"Sure. Sure, Madge. You play around?"

"Of course not. You know I don't."

"Does Arthur?"

"I don't have to have him at my side every minute. We agreed we both need room to breathe, to be more interesting to each other. I trust him." Madge's fingernails raked her hair.

"Horseshit," Liz said, "pure horseshit. You couldn't even trust any of us to catch you."

"How long have you been married, Madge?" Lane asked in a quiet voice.

"Twelve years," Madge answered in a whisper.

"I don't see any problems with an agreement like that between people with a good long-term marriage."

"Don't you," Liz said with heavy sarcasm. "How long is the longest you've been with a man, Miss Christianson?"

"Two years."

"So that makes you an expert." She turned to Madge. "I don't know whose idea it was, this room to breathe shit, but when you love somebody you want to share all the important things, and everything's important. How may years do you have, for chrissake, to spread yourself around a bunch of nitwit fad freaks? They just don't have anybody themselves, that's their problem. Room to breathe, my ass. I'd tell Arthur I don't need any more room to breathe, I've done all the breathing I want."

Madge said, almost inaudibly, "I don't know . . . how Arthur would react."

"Ah. And that's the trouble, isn't it, Madge." Liz took a deep swallow of bourbon. "But you'd find *out*, wouldn't you? And you'll never find that answer in astrology or eastern religions. I'd tell him no more free and easy breathing, you'd better be enough for him or you'll break both his balls."

"That's your style, not my style."

It could never be my style either, Diana thought.

"You have to *fight* for what you love, for what's yours."

I've never fought for anything, Diana thought.

Madge said slowly, deliberately, "You lost."

"At least I *fought*, goddammit!"

"You might have won without fighting. George might never have left if you'd turned your back for a while."

"Maybe. Maybe. And maybe he'd have just broken my back too, like—" She broke off, staring at Madge with glittering dark eyes.

Then she continued in a soft cruel voice, "What's it like, Madge, when he waves it right under your nose? How can you let him put his cock in you when he's putting it in everybody else?"

"When you love somebody enough—"

I could never love anybody enough, Diana thought.

"Shit, Madge." Liz's voice was suddenly heavy, tired. "If what you give him isn't enough let him go fuck himself. It isn't worth it."

"I've got Arthur. It doesn't matter about the terms. And one of these days he'll be old. And with me."

Dear God, Diana thought, her stomach wrenching.

"Let's go on," Madge said softly. "Let me make my statement about Millie."

"Should we really go on with this," Lane said quietly.

Liz said truculently, "Why not? It's not for you to say this isn't helping some of us."

Diana could no longer smell the fresh sharpness of the fire; the cabin reeked of the sweetish smell of marijuana.

"Once we work through the negatives, all the positives will come out," Madge said. Her voice was tired; her face was pale and lined with fatigue. "Millie," she said, turning to her, "I'd like to see you be less naive about people. You think they're all so good and honest, and they're not. I'd like to see you approach your relationships with some skepticism, for your own good."

"What Madge means," Liz said heavily, "is you ought to take off that sign that says fuck me and then kick me." She lurched slightly and caught herself; Diana saw that she was drunk.

"You're wrong, both of you," Millie said. "I'm very skeptical. When you've been hurt as much as me— But every time I meet somebody who seems nice I'm like you, Madge. I think this is the time it'll be different. And for a while it's always really good. And then it changes, and I can't keep it from becoming . . . awful."

"It always changes," Liz said, "that's what you don't understand. The romance always fades, he stops sending flowers and carrying you into the bedroom. That's when you've got to be your own person, be attractive as a person, be more than just a pretty body he enjoys screwing. You can't hold anybody by turning into a nag and a whining baby, Millie. Men want a woman, not a baby."

"I'm not a baby," Millie said with a pout. "Just because I don't wear hobnailed boots like you doesn't mean I don't want to be accepted for what I am, not what somebody else wants."

"Jesus Christ," Liz hissed. "I can understand why men stomp all over you. I've got an almost irresistible urge right now to kick you in the teeth."

"You're just a miserable unhappy old hag."

"Well, well." Liz's smile was wide. "I finally got a little nastiness out of our sweet quiet innocent baby Millie. Is this the first time, Millie? Did I bust your cherry?"

"You hateful bitch!"

"Keep working on it. Maybe someday one man too many'll play you for a doormat and get his feet bitten off."

"Stop this, Liz," Chris slurred. "Stop this right now."

"I'm not a doormat!" Millie glared at Liz. "You'd think that about any woman who just tries to be nice and please men."

Liz shrugged contemptuously. "Have it your way. Maybe you like to be fucked and kicked. I've seen stranger things. Who's next?"

Madge sighed heavily. "You are. This isn't going at all the way it should, but if we just get through it— You make a statement now about Lane."

"What an interesting opportunity." Liz looked speculatively at Lane. "Is there any rule that says I can't skip my turn? I want to think about this."

Madge looked at Liz, alarmed and uncertain. Liz said, "Besides, I'd like to hear what negative Miss Mar-lane-a Christianson has to offer about perfect Diana."

Diana did not look up. Anguished, torn, battered by what she had heard, she sat waiting for another blow to fall, this time from Lane. She stared at the carpet, a deep coldness in her.

"I have nothing negative to say about Diana," Lane said.

"How noble," Liz said scornfully. "Come on," she goaded, "there must be something. Some little thing. How she files her fingernails. Some small thing."

"There's nothing. Everything I know about Diana so far I like. There isn't anything about her I want to see changed."

"Sweet, perfect Diana. How wonderful it must be—to be so sweet and perfect. And attractive along with it. It's so high-minded of you to watch over her. Very high-minded indeed. Dear Diana is down right now about her friend Jack, but Mar-lane-a isn't going to kick her."

Speechless, paralyzed with shock at having her pain exposed in this roomful of strangers, Diana stared helplessly at Liz.

"That's enough," Lane said coldly.

"Vivian told me about you, Diana dear. Or at least what she guessed. We have something in common, dear. You walked out on him just like I did, you know just how it feels. You don't talk about how he hurt you, but the footprints are all over you. You're much too honest, that's your trouble, my dear." Liz's voice was low and harsh. "You need a little more deceit in you when it comes to men. You need that for survival. Men are such bastards. All we want to do is love them and they're such bastards. How could he do any better than you? A little younger maybe, but that's all. Maybe he found somebody who looked like your friend Lane here, all blonde and pretty."

"I said that's enough." Lane's voice was glacial. "And I mean that's enough."

The two women stared in silence. Diana could not see Lane's face; Liz, eyes fixed burningly on Lane, nostrils flared, wide thick lips twisted in hate, said with quiet malevolence, "All right, let's talk about you. I'll take my turn now, Madge. What you need to change is your thinking you're so bloody superior. Woman with a mission, our fair-haired dedicated young lawyer out to save the world with people like Diana sitting at your feet. Shit," she spat, "who needs you?"

"Shut up!" Diana's voice broke from her. She was rigid with fury. "Shut up!"

"It's all right, Diana," Lane said, looking at her briefly, her face calm.

"She's drunk, Lane." Diana wanted to tear at Liz, pummel her with her fists.

"No, my dear, just stoned," Liz said. "There's a world of difference. You piss-ant wine drinkers could take a bath in the amount of bourbon I can put away. George taught me how to drink. Among other things. But George liked me the way I was, too. He married me when he was thirty, after two other marriages and hundreds of other women. For twenty years he wanted me, only me. I know that as sure as I breathe. He used to call me the fastest come in the West . . ." She picked up her drink as the women stirred uneasily.

"One of the boys," Liz said softly. "He always said I was like one of the boys. One of the boys. I reminded him about that when he wanted to be with her. I told him I knew why he smoked those big cigars, why he was always asking to fuck me in the ass. I took this cabin away, I wanted George to know how it feels to get fucked in the ass. One of the boys." Liz chuckled, and Diana grimaced with pain at the sound. "That's what I told that blonde chippy at his office, that slim little blonde. I told her right in front of George and everybody I hoped she liked getting fucked in her little blonde ass every night."

In a flash of understanding Diana blurted, "Lane reminds you of the woman who took your husband away, doesn't she."

Liz stared at Lane. "Tell me dear. Honestly now. Do blondes really have more fun? Do you really have more and better orgasms than the rest of us?"

"Liz," Chris said in her slurred voice. She sat slumped, her head nodding.

"Oh shut up, Chris," Liz said wearily, and drank bourbon.

"I understand your pain," Lane said.

"Do you," Liz said in a low vicious tone, turning on her. "Do you really understand, pretty blonde lady? What do you know? Have you ever lost anybody?"

"Yes."

"I don't believe you. You take anything you want. You've got those looks and brains besides. How could you lose anybody?"

"By not making him go to Canada. I could have made him go, even though he insisted it would complicate our lives too much, he'd just do his tour in the war and get out. And then do you know what happened, Liz?"

"Don't, Lane, don't," Diana whispered, horrified.

But Lane and Liz were leaning toward each other, eyes locked. The fire crackled loudly in the still room. Lane said, "He stepped on a mine where there weren't supposed to be any mines. They found a few pieces of Mark's body for us to bury."

Liz sat swaying, her eyes closed. Diana gazed at Lane through tear-blurred eyes.

Lane said, "It was a long time ago. Years ago, now. A lot of women did what I did. Your man is still alive. He's fifty years old and from what I understand a lot of men his age have a serious affair, one final fling, then go back to their wives. If I were you, that's something

I'd consider, and you're a bigger fool than I think you are if you don't take him back if you get the chance. And I don't think you're a fool."

"It hurts too much," Liz mumbled, her eyes still closed.

"All of us have pain," Lane said. "Some of us can recover from it." She rose to her feet. "I've had enough."

Madge said, "It isn't right to leave it like this. We've worked all through the negatives now. If we stay and talk, all the positives will come out. We'll be just like sisters when we're through."

"I believe you Madge, but I'm still going to bed. Diana, I wish you'd come too."

Diana rose to her feet. Chris said thickly, "Do you realize it's two o'clock?"

"We're skiing tomorrow, too," Millie said. "I want to ski while we still have good snow."

"We're not kids anymore, Liz," mumbled Chris. "Come on, Liz." She helped her sister to her feet and said blearily to the group, "Why don't you let us have the bathroom first."

The two sisters weaved unsteadily down the hallway, supporting each other.

on't get up, I'll take care of us." Lane pulled up the ladder and dropped the trapdoor into place. Diana lay in bed staring unseeingly out the window, her senses numbed and battered.

"An elephant is a good description for Liz," Lane said quietly as she hung her clothes in the closet. "A wounded elephant. Incredibly strong and in great pain and just stumbling around bewildered, trampling things, striking out at anything, trying somehow to deal with it. She's blinded by her pain."

Diana was aware that Lane was standing beside the bed looking down at her. On the edge of tears, Diana did not take her eyes from the window.

Lane blew out the lamp, got into bed. She asked softly, bending over her, "Diana, are you all right?"

"Yes," Diana said tightly.

"Are you sure?"

"Yes."

"I'm not that sure you are."

"I'm okay. Good night."

Diana lay rigidly, emotions sweeping her in warm waves, each wave weakening her further, trying to prevent tears and failing that, trying to stop them. Lane lay unmoving; Diana could not hear her breathing.

Involuntarily, Diana made a gasping sound as hot tears streamed down her face, and Lane said, "I knew you would be like this. You would have to be."

To her intense mortification, Diana began to sob, and Lane

moved to her. "Let me hold you," she said, and took her into her arms.

"I'm sorry," Diana cried into her shoulder.

"Just cry. It's okay. It's the best thing for you to do."

She clung to Lane, weeping, wrung with emotion, each attempt to stop seeming to bring a fresh paroxysm. "I just don't do this," she wept, her body in Lane's arms wracked with sobs.

"It's all right, Diana, it's all right." Lane held her gently, her face against Diana's hair.

After a while her sobs diminished, and she managed to say in an almost normal voice, "I've made your pajama top all wet."

"It'll dry." Lane held her face in her hands and brushed tears away with her fingers. She touched her cheek to Diana's face and rubbed moisture off with her warm skin.

"I'm not even the one who should be crying," Diana said, her voice choking again with tears. "I'm so sorry about Mark."

"Please don't cry for me." Lane's hands held her face gently; her eyes were closed.

"I can't stand to think of the pain you've had."

"It was a long time ago and I'm much better about it now."

"And then to lose your father. Sometimes it seems like all the love in the world has no power to change anything. There was so much pain down there tonight. Does everybody have that kind of pain?"

"At some time or other."

Diana closed her eyes; they stung and burned. "I guess . . . I'm through crying." Reluctantly she added, "I need a Kleenex."

Lane's hands released her face, and Diana sat up and reached to the nightstand. She dabbed at her eyes and blew her nose energetically, looking at the stains of her tears, dark patches in the starlight, on Lane's pajamas, and feeling more and more foolish. "I'm sorry," she said.

"Don't be. Please don't feel that way."

Diana lay back on the bed. "I guess I'm just a big baby," she said, turning to Lane, trying to smile.

Cool fingers touched Diana's face, brushing her hair back. Lane said, "We didn't know what we were doing down there. Women can't tough each other out, we aren't any good at that. We don't know how. We don't get enough practice." Lane's fingertips stroked her forehead and traced down over her cheekbones. "And you're much too sensitive and feeling a woman to be involved in those kinds of games."

Diana looked at her with overwhelming awareness of her beauty, a beauty intensified by shadows and starlight. In the silver light of their room her eyes were a deep gray, her lips a sensual curve, her face a lustrous, austere sculpture of contours and shadows. Blonde hair was tumbled and lying thickly on the pillow. Lane was stroking Diana's hair and stopped; she rolled strands in her fingers and watched Diana look at her. Diana's eyes closed as Lane pulled her face toward her.

"Okay now?" Lane asked softly.

"Okay now," Diana whispered, her eyes still closed. She thought their lips had touched, barest feather-light contact.

"I'll hold you till you sleep, okay?"

"Yes," Diana said, wanting the gentleness of her again.

Lane's body felt almost inconsequentially slender in her arms. She held her face against Lane's throat, feeling strands of hair on her cheek, and she breathed a fragrance intricate and delicate from her hair and skin. Diana lay quietly, aware of pliant breasts that pressed softly against her with Lane's breathing. Lips touched for a moment on her forehead, a melting softness. Diana tightened her arms and turned her face into Lane, brushing her lips over her throat, over silky smooth softness, against the hollow of her throat, feeling the pulse beat.

Then it seemed so very easy, so natural for Diana simply to raise her face and feel the melting softness of Lane's mouth with her own. Her mind vibrating with alarm, she drew away; but Lane's mouth came to hers. Their lips met again and again with tender, brief kisses that became lingering and still more tender, and Lane held her gently, closely. Diana was warm in her arms, her body softening with release; and she yielded as in a dream, her lips parting; and Lane's mouth became the most exquisite velvet, and they kissed deeply, slowly, endlessly, unhurriedly.

Diana lay across Lane's body, sifting the silk of her hair again and again through her fingers. Lane's arms were around her, hands slowly caressing her shoulders. They were kissing deeply. Faint, intermittent sound intruded insistently and assumed coherence: women's voices and the vibration of footsteps. Reluctantly, Diana drew her mouth away, pushed aside the blanket that covered them in the cold of their room, and opened her shocked eyes to daylight. Lane's arms tightened, and Diana said very quietly, "It's time for you to put on ski clothes."

Eyes shut tight against the light, Lane murmured indecipherably and reached up and drew the blanket over them again, and dissolved all Diana's thought with her mouth.

Some time later, they heard Liz's shout from below, "Hey up there!"

Lane's arms released Diana, but she held her face with gentle fingers for moments longer and her mouth left hers only slowly. She traced a finger across Diana's cheek. "We'd better get down there," she said softly, and sat up. But she stared unmoving, out the window at the Lake.

Diana rubbed her eyes and said, choosing her words hesitantly, "Thank you for . . . for being here . . . for . . . for what I needed."

Lane said, "I'm glad we could be together." She leaned her head back, shaking her hair, then got up and donned her robe and slippers, and opened the trapdoor, sliding the ladder down. "Give me seven minutes in the bathroom," she said, with the briefest of glances at Diana as she climbed down.

Diana absently selected pants and a sweater, and went to the window. She felt tired but relaxed, almost languid. She thought it had been very good for her to cry; she had needed to. She stared at the blinding white snow and the distant glistening blue of Lake Tahoe, her mind blank, emptied of thought.

A few minutes later she nodded and said good morning to the group drinking coffee around the fire, and went into the bathroom and closed the door, leaning against it with her eyes closed, breathing the lingering fragrance of Lane's perfume. She brushed her hair with long, automatic strokes, arranging the soft waves with pats of her hand as she always did, looking intently into the mirror, examining herself as she would a peculiar but fascinating stranger. She splashed cold water on her face.

When she came out of the bathroom she watched Lane climb gracefully down the ladder dressed in her royal blue ski clothes, blonde hair swaying and changing its patterns with her movements. Diana pulled her gaze away and went into the kitchen and poured coffee, and joined the group at the fireplace.

All the women were dressed for skiing. Their conversation was sporadic, forced, subdued. Diana realized she had completely forgotten the events of the previous night, the disastrous disintegration of the encounter games. The women were solemn, thoughtful, evading each other's eyes.

"Anybody as hung over as I am?" Liz asked, grimacing as she massaged the back of her neck.

"I am dying, Egypt, dying," Madge intoned, clutching her head.

"I feel fine," Millie said.

"I'm getting too old for this," Liz sighed. "George and I used to party all night at the clubs and then go skiing without even going to bed. We could do it in those days. Today I'll consider it a penance."

"I hope just for your hangover, Liz," Lane said. "No other damage was done as far as I'm concerned."

The two women looked at each other with a gaze that was lengthy and unflinching.

"Good," Liz said, nodding.

"We've been friends for years," Madge said. "It'll take a lot more than just one evening with all of us smashed on booze and grass to change that."

Millie said, "We know each other so well. Friends are too hard to find."

"There were some good things too, last night," Chris said.

"Yes," Diana said, knowing that some statement, however brief, was expected of her.

Liz said, "Good friends, let's have breakfast."

Diana pushed at her scrambled eggs, pricklingly aware of Lane. Lane finished her breakfast quickly and sat drinking coffee, staring out the window, seeming to have no awareness of Diana.

The women left for the ski slopes. Diana drove to Harrah's.

She sat in her car in the parking lot, fingering her keys, head back against the headrest, looking at the white mountains, and thought of her own femininity, the femininity of Lane—the elegance of her gestures, her movements, her clothes.

What had happened between them was inexplicable. But with astonishing ease she constructed an image of Lane's beauty adorned by the simplicity of jeans and a white shirt, and she was pierced by the beauty of the image. Disturbed, she pushed this forcibly from her mind, reminding herself that she had never been physically attracted to a woman in her life. Defiantly, easily, she conjured up her favorite fantasy of a beautiful man in a white silk shirt, his hands and his mouth tender on her . . .

As she got out of the car she reminded herself with a trace of self-pity that she had been a long time without sex, nearly two months.

She waited until she was almost across the parking lot to admit the pleasure of the night before. She had not wanted the night to end; she had loved Lane's touch; and much of her pleasure had been savoring the knowledge that Lane had enjoyed her mouth, her arms, her body.

It was different. That was all, she told herself. She had had more wine than usual—but with satisfaction she considered that neither she nor Lane had made the easy, dishonest suggestion that wine had contributed to their night together. Deep emotion had surfaced in both of them from the encounter games. And Lane had protected her from that cruel, pathetic, drunken woman. And she liked Lane, liked her very much.

She walked into Harrah's uncomfortable with her last thought. She knew that *like* was not precisely what she felt for Lane.

Across the street at Harvey's she found Vivian, bleary-eyed, dispiritedly pulling the handle of a dollar slot machine.

"How's it going, Viv?" Diana's spirits rose at the sight of her. The world seemed suddenly more normal.

"Terrible. John gave me another hundred and practically ordered me to make it last." She added with a crafty grin, "Till Vivian can get him back in bed."

Diana laughed. "Dollar slot machines aren't recommended for making your money last, you know." She gazed at Vivian with affection.

"I know, I know. But maybe I'll hit something. If not, I'll just go up to the room and sleep. I could use some." She dropped another dollar into her machine. "Diana dear, Vivian needs a favor. You can do it for me. Will you?"

"Sure. What is it?"

"Call Fred at the office and tell him you want one more day off. You know it won't be any problem. They love us to take vacation this time of year instead of summer when everybody wants to go. I want to stay another day. Say yes, Diana."

She considered quickly. This meant that they would leave Thursday. Lane would be leaving Wednesday anyway.

Vivian said, "I know Liz won't mind having you stay another day. If you don't want to stay there I'll pay for a motel. At least I think I will." She looked balefully at her machine.

"I love the cabin," Diana said. "I'm sure Liz won't mind, either." She knew Liz would welcome a chance to atone for her behavior.

"You'll stay?"

"Sure. What are friends for?"

"You're a dear. I'll take you to breakfast."

"I've had breakfast."

"Stupid me. I forgot those fabulous ranch-hand breakfasts Liz whips up. I wish George hadn't ruined everything. It was wonderful when the two of them were together."

"So I gather," Diana said drily.

Three symbols settled across the center of Vivian's slot machine. Diana jumped as Vivian shrieked. The machine lit up and began to ring.

"Three hundred dollars!" Vivian screamed, pointing, her hand trembling. Nearby players regarded her with expressions that ranged from amused smiles to sour-faced resentment. Vivian grabbed Diana and hugged her. "You're my good luck charm! Oh what a great day it's going to be!"

Diana laughed as Vivian again hugged her ecstatically. She helped collect Vivian's winnings as they clattered into the metal tray, the machine ringing interminably. They went off arm in arm to the change booth carrying paper cups full of silver dollars.

Diana, in a pay phone in Harrah's, hung up from her call to Los Angeles. As Vivian had predicted, Fred McPherson had told her in his dry tired voice, "Sure, Diana, no problem. See you Friday."

She watched a girl with lustrous dark hair stroll by her phone booth. She leaned back and closed her eyes and remembered Lane's face against hers, Lane's fingers stroking her hair as if she would never tire of the texture, drawing Diana's hair across her face, bathing her face in it. Diana had shifted her body to lean on her elbows, to brush her hair over Lane's face, her throat. "Yes," Lane had whispered, the only word spoken between them during the night. With Lane's arms around her, she had endlessly brushed and caressed Lane with her hair; and when Lane's arms finally released her, Lane had brushed Diana's face with her own hair: soft, perfumed silkiness caressing Diana's eyelids, her throat. Then Lane's mouth had come to hers . . .

Abruptly, Diana opened the phone booth door and walked into the casino. She paced the length of Harrah's several times, wanting to exercise, use her body. She selected a blackjack table.

"How's your luck running?" she asked the dealer. She had discovered that most dealers answered this question readily.

"Not too bad. Make yourself comfortable." The dealer was young and pretty, a cool-looking brunette with horn-rimmed glasses and a nametag that said Karla.

"How's the winter been?" Diana asked sociably, placing a two dollar bet.

"Depends. How high do you like your snow?"

Diana laughed. She and the dealer chatted amicably but intermittently. Diana occupied her mind with gambling. Her cards ran in patterns—mediocre, or for streaks of eight to ten hands, very good. She played carefully, with concentration, betting her good cards more aggressively than usual. She ran into a series of bad cards, lost six hands in a row. "I'll sit out a round," she told the dealer.

She flexed tight muscles in her shoulders and glanced around and saw a young man and an attractive blonde walking slowly by, heads close together, holding hands. She remembered holding Lane's face in her hands, kissing her; Lane's hands covering hers, taking Diana's hands from her face to kiss her fingers, her palms, inside her wrists. Then Lane had held her hands, their fingers intertwined and caressing, her mouth on Diana's in sweet, slow tenderness . . .

"You in yet?" the dealer asked.

"I guess," Diana said, pushing two silver dollars into the betting square.

"You looked a million miles away."

"Thanks a lot for bringing me back," Diana said wryly. "You just dealt me another fifteen."

"Sorry. Wherever you were, you looked like it was pretty pleasant, too."

"Mmm," Diana said, smiling, signaling for a card.

"There," the dealer said, giving her a four. "What's wrong with that?"

"Is it high enough?" The dealer's upcard was a queen.

The dealer shrugged noncommittally and turned to the player next to Diana, an elderly man smoking a cigar and drinking a vile-looking green concoction. "I get a million miles away, myself," the dealer said. "The customers'd choke if they knew what I think about sometimes."

Diana chuckled, and there was laughter from around the table. The dealer turned over a six and hit her sixteen with a four. "Oops," she said.

Diana picked up her money. "You're getting a little warm. See you later, maybe."

She was having lunch with Vivian when it occurred to her that Lane must also be struggling to understand the previous night. With growing dismay, Diana remembered that she had put an arm around Lane twice when they had looked at the stars; Lane had not touched her. And the next morning she had told Lane she was beautiful. In dawning horror she realized that Lane might think that she was actually a—she swallowed over the word—lesbian. Or bisexual, more accurately. She was suddenly grateful to Liz for exposing her relationship with Jack.

"Are you listening to me?" demanded Vivian.

"Of course. You were talking about your jackpot and how clever you were to hit it."

"You cynic." Vivian chuckled. "You're being awfully quiet, even for you."

Diana smiled. "You talk enough for both of us."

As Vivian resumed her chatter, Diana decided that it was futile to torment herself with speculation. Her night with Lane belonged in the category of just one of those things, and tonight Lane would know that as a certainty.

Vivian said, "Why don't you stay in town and celebrate with John and Vivian tonight?"

"Liz is expecting me."

"Oh, she won't mind. She knows how easy it is to get hung up on gambling."

"I can't tonight," Diana said firmly. She knew her absence would be misinterpreted by Liz; and there was another, more compelling reason for returning to the cabin. After a day with her thoughts she wanted to confront her feelings in the presence of Lane and further diminish them, to assign a final unimportance.

"What about tomorrow then? John and I want to take you somewhere special."

"Tomorrow's just fine."

At the end of the day Diana was slightly over one hundred and fifty dollars ahead. Just before seven, she returned to the cabin.

Liz said, "Everyone's agreed to let me take them out to dinner. I hope you will too, Diana. We'll go into town, get rid of our cabin fever."

"Sure Liz, I'd love to," Diana said, her eyes searching for Lane.

The women were all dressed for dinner in pants and blouses and sweaters; Lane, sitting on the sofa with her feet tucked up under her, wore black pants with a belt of small gold links, a white silk blouse fastened at the throat by a thin silk cord, and tiny gold earrings.

Their eyes met. Lane smiled. Diana smiled in return, and looked away from her, stunned by her beauty. Flustered, she walked into the kitchen, nonplussed by her rapid pulse, a sinking sensation, a feeling of weakness.

Liz followed her. "Pour you some wine? Or how about some vodka?"

"No, I'll just get a glass of water," she murmured. She drank icy cold water slowly, and calmed herself by relating the story of Vivian's jackpot, mentioning also Vivian's request that she stay another day. As she expected, Liz insisted that she remain at the cabin.

She joined the group in the living room, talked again about Vivian's jackpot, her own success at the tables. She said to Liz, "You really ought to let me take everybody on my winnings."

"No way," Liz stated.

"You can lose it back just as easily," Chris said.

"I shouldn't do worse than break even now," Diana said.

"Maybe I should take up gambling," Lane said.

"You?" Madge scoffed.

"Me. Why not?"

"Gambling just doesn't go with that ironclad self-discipline of yours."

"You make me sound perfectly dull," Lane observed in a dispassionate voice.

"I could teach you blackjack, it's the only game I know anything about," Diana said, thinking with an emotion close to amusement that from now on she would have to dress her favorite male fantasy figure in something other than a white silk shirt. She excused herself to change clothes.

She selected green pants and a white cashmere sweater; the soft sweater felt unusually sensual on her skin, especially at the top of her breasts above her bra. She saw Lane's pajamas hanging from a hook in the closet, faint discolorations across the shoulders.

They got into Liz's station wagon, Diana climbing in first, wanting Lane to decide where she would sit. But Liz said, "Lane, sit up here with me."

As the station wagon descended the mountain road, Liz said in a low voice, "It's so lovely here in the summer too, the streams and wildlife. You just get your groceries and stay in the beautiful mountains, away from all the carloads of tourists."

Madge said, "They've been talking about protecting this area for years. Too much politics involved if you want my opinion. Nevada needs money too badly."

"I work with all the groups trying to protect the area," Liz said. "George and I were here when nothing else was and we've seen all the ugliness come." Liz peered over her steering wheel up at the sky. "Could be some snow tonight. Sky looks bad."

Diana murmured, " 'The Sky is low—the Clouds are mean' "

Chris said something Diana did not hear; Lane had turned around, and with her chin resting on her arm she looked back at Diana with a slowly deepening smile that pierced her with its loveliness and intimacy.

They had dinner in the Sage Room at Harvey's. "I've been coming here for twenty years and the food is consistently some of the best at the Lake. Not many things in this life are consistent for twenty years," Liz said.

"True," Lane said. "And there's no awareness of a casino, all that noise just a few feet away."

Lane sat next to Liz; Diana was across from her. Lane seemed relaxed, casual. She sipped occasionally from a vodka and tonic.

Liz said to Lane, "Madge tells me your dad was a lawyer. You catch the law bug from him?"

"Yes. To begin with. There are aspects of it that totally fascinate me." As the women looked at her expectantly, Lane continued, "It's so convoluted, so fluid, so flexible. It's the opposite of mathematics. It's logical, but there's nothing precise or exact about it. It's like water filling up a container and conforming to fit the shape of the container."

"I'm not sure I understand all that but it doesn't matter," Liz said. "You're so sharp and good-looking I know damn well you have to beat the men off. You deliberately avoiding marriage?"

"Liz," Chris protested, "that's a very personal question."

"It's all right." Lane shrugged. "No, I'm not avoiding marriage."

"What the hell are you looking for?"

"Mister Right," Lane said mockingly.

"What's Mister Right like?" Liz persisted.

Diana expected another facetious response, but Lane answered seriously, "Someone I don't dominate. I seem to always end up dominating my male relationships."

Liz gazed at her levelly, with frank appraisal. "I really admire you. You're one steel-strong lady. But I'd sure think twice about taking you on if I were a man, I don't care how good-looking you are. I bet there's a few sadder but wiser male bodies lying around San Francisco."

Lane smiled thinly. "I'm afraid so."

Liz turned to Diana with a grin. "You still think she's gentle and sensitive?"

In a flash of memory Diana thought of Lane's mouth leaving hers to tenderly touch her eyes, under her eyes; her tongue stroking warmly, gently, slowly down her cheeks, washing the traces of tears from her face; Lane's mouth coming back to hers, the taste of salt on her lips, and as Lane's lips parted, the taste of salt on her tongue . . .

"Yes," Diana said.

Liz said to Lane, "You're a complicated woman."

"I don't think so," Lane said.

The waiter brought their salads. "Isn't he cute," Millie giggled, staring at his retreating figure. "I love men with little teeny behinds. Anybody believe in love at first sight?"

"I believe in the possibility of it," Lane said.

"For God's sake I was only kidding," Millie said aggrievedly.

"I have no sense of humor," Lane said.

Diana laughed and looked up at her. Lane's gaze was just leaving her; she thought Lane had been looking at her breasts, but decided she was mistaken. Lane had not touched them during the night; she had held her in her arms, held her face, her hands. Flushed and uncomfortable, Diana remembered her own hands under Lane's pajamas, caressing, savoring warm smoothness and softness. But she had not touched Lane's breasts either; and she looked at them now, thinking that they would fit into her cupped hands, knowing that what she felt was regret. Nothing had really happened between them — and nothing possibly could.

She watched as Lane leaned, smiling, to hear something Madge was telling her in a low tone, and she thought of a statue she had once seen at the Los Angeles County Museum of Art, a statue of a woman carved from such rich warm alabaster and so sensuously curved that she had longed to stroke and caress its lovely feminine lines. She noticed Lane's long slender fingers brushing frost from the glass containing her drink, fingertips stroking back and forth, dissolving the frost. She remembered Lane's fingertips slowly, tenderly stroking her face, her ears, her throat, as they kissed . . . and kissed. . . .

In the surge of eroticism that gripped her she told herself very calmly that in just two more days these strange feelings would leave her; this woman would be gone from her life.

After dinner the women went their separate ways, agreeing to meet at midnight at Harvey's. Diana and Liz went across the street to Harrah's to look for Vivian, and found her at a craps table with John, who looked at Diana leeringly as he always did, and hugged her too tightly, as he always did.

Resisting the desire to go back to Harvey's, to Lane, Diana chose a blackjack table and sat down to play, concentrating on the game with difficulty. She had won five hands in a row and was betting ten dollars when she heard Millie's voice: "Look at that!" With a surge of pleasure she saw Lane and Millie standing behind her.

The chair next to her was empty. "Do you want to play?" she asked Lane. "I can teach you as we go. It's not that hard."

"I'll watch for a while first," Lane said.

"It costs too much," Millie said.

"Less than keno or slot machines most of the time, you'd be surprised." She won her hand, and increased her bet.

"You're betting fifteen dollars!" Millie exclaimed.

"I'm ahead, it's their money I'm betting," Diana explained. "That's how you win. You bet more as you win, as little as you can when you lose."

She won again as the dealer went broke. Lane said, "Would you bet ten dollars on your hand for me?"

"Sure." Diana increased her own bet to twenty dollars and added two five dollar chips for Lane. She drew a nine and a five. The dealer's upcard was a nine. "Sorry," she said to Lane. "The dealer could have nineteen. Fine time for me to get fourteen."

"Do we lose?"

"Not yet. See if we can improve it." She signaled for a card, and to her delight it was a seven.

"Is that as good as I think it is?"

"Worst we can do is tie. What do you want to bet now?"

"Take ten and leave ten?"

"Good."

The dealer did have nineteen, and Diana bet twenty-five of her own money and another ten for Lane. She drew nineteen to the dealer's upcard of ten, and waited tensely as the dealer went around the table to the other players. She finally turned over her hole card, a seven.

"Fantastic," Lane said. "Let the twenty go. I know a winner when I see one."

"Good Lord," Millie gasped, "there's fifty dollars out there!"

"Pretend it's Monopoly money," Diana said. "I do."

Lane laughed. Diana picked up her two cards, an eighteen to the dealer's upcard of three. "Not too bad," she told Lane. The dealer went broke. Diana glanced back to Lane. "I don't care what you say, twenty's the most I'm betting for you. I've been known to lose an occasional hand."

"Whatever you say."

"Not this time," Diana said almost apologetically, turning over an ace and ten. "Guess we should have bet everything. Is twenty okay again?"

"Okay," Lane said, laughing. "This is fantastic."

Diana drew a seventeen, to the dealer's upcard of five; but the dealer drew out to twenty. "Ouch. Is there an Emily Dickinson line that fits?"

Lane laughed. "I don't think she ever played blackjack. How much am I ahead?"

"Fifty. Sit out a hand, okay? These things are usually over when they're over." She bet two dollars.

"What a comedown from seventy dollars," Millie said.

Diana lost as the dealer drew out to twenty-one. "I see what you mean," Lane said. "What's the most you've ever bet?"

"About fifty dollars, on a really good streak." Diana lost the next two hands as well, and Millie wandered off, saying she wanted to play keno.

Diana felt Lane's hand, warm through the cashmere of her sweater, smelled her perfume. "The woman at the end of the table," Lane said in a low tone close to her ear, "how much is she betting?"

Diana glanced at a sharp-featured woman of perhaps thirty, wearing a simple beige wool dress, who was settling herself on a stool. She had placed four black chips in her betting square. "Four hundred," she murmured to Lane who was bent over close to her. "Watch the man next to her." She had noticed him add four five dollar chips to his original ten dollar bet.

She murmured again, after several hands had been played, "Four hundred's her standard bet, but see how he chases his money?"

"What do you mean?" Lane asked softly, close to her.

"He's losing, and betting more and more."

Diana played absently, making minimum bets as she watched the man and woman, and she murmured commentary to Lane, inhaling perfume, acutely aware of her nearness.

The man finally got up. "She's too lucky for me," he said to the woman.

"Yeah," the woman said indifferently. "See you around. Better luck." She pushed four more black chips into her betting square.

The man left, with a final backward glance. The woman lost her hand, and picked up her purse, a simple leather bag. "Baccarat's really my game," she said to no one in particular. "Thank you dear, I enjoyed it," she said to the dealer, handing her two green chips. She moved quickly away, disappearing in the casino crowd.

"Fifty bucks!" The dealer stared in astonishment at the green chips in her palm. "And I took her for three thousand!"

Diana picked up her money. "I played longer than I should have just watching her. I wonder what she'd give you if she won."

The dealer's grin was rueful. "Don't rub it in."

Diana handed Lane her winnings, a stack of five dollar chips.

"Free money," Lane said, hefting the chips. "How very strange. Let me buy you a drink. Or would you prefer to play more?"

"A drink would be fine."

They paused at the cabaret area, its stage curtained between shows. "I think there's a cover charge if we sit in there," Diana said.

"It looks comfortable," Lane said firmly.

"You have the makings of a gambler," Diana told Lane as their drinks arrived. She touched her glass to hers in salute.

"Do you think so," Lane said, smiling, playing with her chips, piling them in two stacks beside her vodka and tonic. "You seem to be very good at it." She added, "Very courageous."

"I was more or less compelled to learn. Actually, I get pretty bored after a couple of days. Tonight was fun. I can entertain myself just watching the people. Like that woman at our table. How can anyone be so indifferent to money?"

"She didn't have a piece of jewelry on her, not even a ring."

"Isn't that odd. I see men bet sums like she did, but not many women. A few years ago I saw a woman betting five hundred dollars a hand, playing three hands. It was in the wee small hours and she was at a table by herself with quite a group watching. She looked like an old maid school teacher. She had about forty thousand dollars in front of her, she looked cool as a cucumber—except for one foot tapping like a drumbeat. I saw her the next day betting two dollars. Makes you wonder, doesn't it?"

Lane, arms crossed on the table, was leaning toward her, smiling, listening with lively interest. "What a strange and different world."

"Yes." Diana was enjoying her attention. "The people fascinate me. Don't you wonder about that woman tonight? Where does she get that money? Why did she bet like that? Was it an act, a show? Or were those four hundred dollar bets like two dollars for us?"

"I don't think it was a show."

"I don't either, somehow. A woman betting like that, a fifty dollar tip for the dealer—it did my heart good. I felt proud of her."

Lane smiled. "I know exactly what you mean. That man next to her, he lost a lot of money—for him."

"Did he ever. He was betting ten dollars before she sat down. I always notice what people bet. I imagine he lost a good part of his gambling money trying to impress a woman who couldn't have cared less."

"Gambling seems to have its own special kind of insanity."

"It can. It depends on—"

The waitress arrived with two more drinks. "From the two gentlemen over there at the corner table."

"We don't want this, do we?" Lane asked without a glance where the waitress indicated.

"Absolutely not."

Lane took two five dollar chips off her stack and placed them on the waitress's tray. "Please take them back. Could you see to it that we're not disturbed?"

"I know just how to take care of it," the waitress said.

"Are you always such a big spender or have you been taking lessons?" Diana teased.

"Natural talent," Lane said with a grin.

There was an awkward silence. Diana looked at the table, and then away as she saw Lane's fingers begin to brush frost from her glass.

"Is everything okay with you, Diana?" Lane's voice was quiet.

Diana nodded, and with effort, met her eyes. "How about you?"

"Yes, okay. I'm fine."

"It was . . . a very emotional night."

"Yes, I've been concerned about you. You seemed upset at dinner. I want to be sure you feel okay about . . . everything."

"I appreciate that. You're an unusual person," Diana said with feeling.

"So are you. You're a very special person—" Lane started as the stage curtain rose to a blare of sound. "This won't do," she said. "Unless you want to stay?"

"No."

"Good." Lane smiled. "I have a weak head. Noise makes it ache."

"We'd better hurry then," Diana said to a thunder of drumbeats.

As they made their way through the tables Diana heard a man say to his male companion, "Those two sure don't look like Carmelite nuns to me."

Diana and Lane made it to the casino area before they burst into laughter.

Liz came up to them. "I've been looking all over for you. Chris doesn't feel well. I think she's just overtired, but I'd better get her back to the cabin. I can pick you up later if you want to give me a time."

"Do you want to play more?" Lane asked Diana.

"I'm sure everyone's tired," Diana said. "Why don't we go on back?"

The air was still, bitterly cold, and Diana shivered as they walked to the station wagon, her hands plunged deeply into her jacket pockets.

"One of us should have brought the car around," Lane said, looking at her.

"I'm okay," Diana said, annoyed with herself. "It's just my thin Southern California blood."

"The wagon heats up fast," Liz said.

"I understand from Millie that you and Diana are a pair of high rollers," Liz said. She and Lane chatted as Liz drove swiftly down Highway 50, Liz's arm across the seat behind Lane. Chris, next to Lane, lay back, eyes closed, her face pale.

As Lane told Liz about the woman gambler, Diana watched her. Lane's face was in profile, her beauty sharp-edged simplicity, her hair highlighted with gold by bright neon and headlights.

She thought over their conversation. Very clearly, Lane had told her she assigned no special significance to any behavior of Diana's, or to their night together. Diana remembered Lane's statements during the encounter games describing some relationships as butterfly interludes; and with an odd mixture of relief and depression she realized that Lane obviously thought of their night together as somewhat less than even a butterfly interlude.

"False alarm about the storm," Liz said, peering up over her steering wheel as they wound their way up the mountain road.

"Yes," Lane said. "All the stars are out."

Chris went immediately to bed. Liz poked the fire into vigorous life, and the cabin became quickly comfortable. The women began their preparations for bed.

Lane was standing by the window when Diana stepped into the room. Diana pulled up the ladder and lowered the trapdoor, deciding firmly that she would not go to her.

She got into bed and lay with an arm across her eyes, thinking that she did not want to talk, or think, or feel. She did not want to continue their interrupted conversation, to have Lane further diminish their night of tenderness and pleasure. She only wanted Lane to get into bed and say good night and fall asleep.

Lane turned from the window finally, and blew out the lamp. She got into bed, the silence between them stretching out with wire-drawn tension. There was the scent of perfume. Diana opened her eyes as Lane bent to her.

"Diana," whispered Lane.

"Yes," Diana answered, reaching for her, her hands and then her arms feeling the warmth of Lane's body through the cool silk of her pajamas.

"Diana," Lane whispered again, and her mouth was more meltingly tender than Diana had remembered, had been remembering all day.

Diana held Lane's face between her hands and kissed across her forehead and into her hair; her lips brushed the curving line of eyebrow and moved very gently over delicate eyelids, her tongue touching long thick eyelashes. Diana's lips explored the planes of

Lane's face as her fingertips traced the intricacy of her ears and the shape of her nose, feeling the warmth of Lane's breath on her fingers. She felt her lips with her own, touching the corners with her tongue, and then felt them again, kissing slowly across them; soft, tender lips that did not answer hers, sensing her wish to simply feel their shape. Then she laid her face against Lane's throat, and with her fingertips touching Lane's face, she said in a muffled whisper, "Why must you be so very beautiful."

After a moment Lane said, "For you," and she kissed Diana's fingers.

Blindly, Diana raised her face and felt Lane's lips again, this time answering, tenderly moving against her lips, parting softly. Diana moved into her arms, seeking her, Lane's arms enclosing her as their kiss deepened.

Leaning on her elbows, Lane unfastened Diana's pajama top and opened it; and her hands held Diana's bare shoulders. Hair falling over her forehead, face in shadow, she looked at Diana's breasts for a long moment, and then laid her face on them, and Diana held Lane's face to her, stroking her hair.

Lane kissed the hollows of her shoulders; and then her slim fingers circled Diana's breasts. She brushed her hair across them, caressed them slowly with her face, touched and explored them with gentle, sensuous fingers. Diana's hands were in her hair as Lane's mouth came to her breasts and kissed in warm, slow circles until with a murmur of pleasure that blended with Diana's soft Oh, she took a nipple into her mouth. Diana's throat tightened, ached from the sweetness of Lane's mouth. When Lane at last took her mouth away she unbuttoned the top of her own pajamas and laid her breasts on Diana's, softness on softness.

Diana cupped Lane's breasts in her hands, and she put her face in them, between them, holding the softness against her; her lips moved over their smooth richness. A searing thought passed through her: no wonder men love us so. She touched a nipple with her tongue, slowly tasted it, felt it become swollen tautness from light swirls of her tongue as Lane made a murmuring sound and her body stirred, her hands in Diana's hair holding her mouth to her.

Lane kissed Diana's breasts again. Once she murmured, "Am I doing this too much," and Diana said from out of her pleasure, "No, it's wonderful." Lane kissed her face, her throat, her shoulders; gentle hands moved slowly on Diana's body, caressing down her hips; warm hands creating excitement, desire; warm hands caressing, stroking her thighs. Lane's mouth came to Diana's breasts again and again, and pleasure swept Diana from every touch of her mouth, her nipples electric under Lane's tongue, her body filled with pleasure like sweet, slow-moving honey.

She gasped from fingers touching lightly, gently inside her thighs, and pleasure and desire came together and focused intensely, powerfully. Her body surged against Lane, her breath coming quickly, her body trembling as Lane's hands began to pull down her pajamas.

"No," Diana said, her voice choked. Struggling, shaking with desire, her body like a flame, she pulled away from Lane and lay on her stomach, breathing with effort, her heart pounding. She said haltingly, "I can't . . . I don't . . . I'm not . . . ."

"Don't explain, Diana."

"Lane—"

"Don't explain."

She felt Lane get out of bed, moments later heard the door to the other room roll back. She lay quietly, hurting with every breath she drew. The want in her body gradually became a vague ache that never fully disappeared, but she finally fell asleep, exhausted.

Diana awoke to Lane's voice saying her name.

Lane sat tensely on the side of the bed, wearing her ski clothes. "I wanted to let you sleep as long as you could," she said quietly. "Breakfast is almost ready. Liz will be insulted if you don't show the proper degree of enthusiasm for her food." She smiled tiredly.

Diana was penetrated by a desire to hold her, caress and soothe her, a desire so urgent that she clenched her hands. She said tightly, "I won't be back tonight."

"Don't do this," Lane said, closing her eyes.

"I have to. I can't even . . . be around you. I can't—"

"Don't say any more." Lane got up and went to the ladder and climbed down without looking up.

Diana picked at her breakfast, forcing herself to eat. She and Lane were both silent, but the other women, chattering among themselves, appeared not to notice.

"By the way, Liz," Diana said in a voice that sounded strange to her, "I'm staying in town tonight, having dinner with Vivian and John, and—"

Liz held up a hand. "Fine, fine, I'll give you a key. If you're really late you can sleep on the sofa." She added with a grin, "Gentle and sensitive Lane'll probably pull the ladder up, anyway."

Diana smiled with painful effort, feeling Lane's eyes on her.

Buffeted by vivid memory, her body weak and warm, she stood at the window watching Lane arrange ski equipment in the station wagon, her gold hair blowing in the wind. Lane glanced at the cabin, saw Diana and stood looking at her, a hand shading her eyes. She turned and got into the station wagon.

A few minutes later, Diana sat in her car in Harrah's parking lot, smiling bitterly over her easy answers of yesterday. Getting out of the car, she told herself that now it was even simpler: she would never see Lane Christianson again. The insanity would go away.

She repeated over and over as she walked to the casino: I am not a lesbian. I am not a lesbian. I am *not*.

She found Vivian at Harvey's. Vivian looked at her in distress. "Diana! Honey! What's wrong?"

"Nothing," Diana said, alarmed.

"Yes, there is. I *know* you. Tell me what's wrong, Diana."

She answered in her mind: Only a woman who makes me weak when I look at her and makes me fall apart when she touches me. Diana almost smiled, imagining Vivian's reaction.

"Has Liz been at you again? She told me last night what a mess she made, how terrible she was."

"Liz has been terrific."

"She feels dreadful, you have no idea. It's Jack, isn't it. You've had another bad night over that useless, undeserving—"

"You're so perceptive," Diana said gratefully.

"I thought it would be such a good idea to come up here and get your mind off him."

"It was a very good idea," Diana said ironically.

She tried to play blackjack but could not concentrate. Instead, she strolled through the casino, looking at women, lingering over attractive women, gazing at them, imagining them touching her, kissing her. She felt not the slightest response—a dry triumph. She had not expected to.

She contemplated the close female relationships in her life. She had stayed overnight with girlfriends when she was in her preteens, and there had been the intense friendship with Margaret Benjamin when she was fourteen. The greatest likelihood for a lesbian affair had surely existed with Barbara Nichols. In their year and a half together, she had seen Barbara naked many times—with no emotion other than a guilty satisfaction in the superiority of her own body. They must surely have touched at times, Diana reflected; but she could remember no specific occasion nor any unusual emotion.

Uncomfortably, she remembered how good it had been to be

with Barbara. The evenings of tranquil companionship with a woman intuitive of her moods and needs, who gave gentle ministration to her self-doubts and depressions. Then she had met Jack, Barbara had married and moved to Phoenix. But it had been good to be with her, a time of peace. She had recovered from the destructive, turbulent years of her marriage. Barbara had healed her.

She walked into the keno area thinking of a short story she had read recently, *Death in Venice,* and the man Aschenbach who had become obsessed with a beautiful young boy after a long life of conventionality. She had to leave Lake Tahoe, she decided, and this one-time aberration would go away.

Absently, she began to mark a keno ticket. Anger rose and sharpened as she reflected that she had done nothing to deserve this, had not sought this. She had loved the tenderness of Lane, that was all. She had wanted the tenderness again last night. But *she* had turned it into something else, *she* had made her want more and more.

She stood utterly still as a thought struck: Lane had been with women before. Drawing aimless patterns on her keno ticket, she swiftly considered the evidence: Lane's acceptance of her approach their first night. The building sexuality, the incredible pleasure she had felt last night—Lane knew how to touch, to please a woman. And she lived in San Francisco, a city with many women who wanted other women.

How could she have been so stupid? She thought of Lane's approval of butterfly interludes, her cool acknowledgement to Liz of the bodies she had left lying around San Francisco. Lane had never married. How convenient—when the bodies were male and female. Bitterly, she thought of how close she had come to being one of those bodies—the length of time it would have taken Lane to pull her pajamas down over her hips. She crumpled her keno ticket in a pure white flash of rage.

She stalked from the casino into the brilliant early spring sunlight, and strode several blocks with her hands clenched at her sides, glaring at the ground. She crossed the street, and in the length of time it took to walk back to Harrah's, her anger had turned to self-accusation. She herself was the one who had caused this mess. She had made their physical relationship happen. Lane had not approached her. A woman like her would not make approaches. No, *she* was the one who had changed everything—she had come to Lane.

And she had destroyed the possibility of friendship with this admirable, unusual woman for whom she had felt such affinity and closeness.

She sat at a blackjack table, and ten minutes later had lost fifty dollars. Recognizing this as useless self-flagellation, she left the table and wandered aimlessly, miserable with her thoughts, condemning herself for encouraging a woman to touch her. Lane had been honest; she had not. She had wanted Lane—she flushed, remembering how clearly she had communicated that want. She called herself a tease—behavior she despised in other women. She had acted despicably toward a woman who had comforted her, given her pleasure emotionally and physically. In anguish Diana thought: I've hurt a tender, sensitive woman . . . and I'll never see her again.

She walked into a keno area and sat in one of the chairs and remembered Lane, her body dissolving with weakness.

"Hey daydreamer," Vivian said. "Why don't we go down to the Sahara for a change of scenery?"

"Good idea," Diana said.

With Vivian at her side chattering continuously, her thoughts became harsh again. Lane had known exactly how to be with her. The tenderness was an act, a fraud—just like those five years with Jack Gordon when she had been convinced that she was the one and only woman in his life.

"I've gone sour on slots," Vivian said. "Why don't we try something different? How about a little roulette?"

"Sure," Diana said indifferently.

Vivian lost quickly, spreading her yellow chips all over the roulette layout. "Whose lousy idea was this anyway," she grumbled, getting up to leave.

"I'll play the rest of mine," Diana said.

The young man who sat down in Vivian's chair was tall, with broad shoulders in a good tweed jacket, and a compact, athletic body. His hair was sand-colored and thinning, his features well-defined and handsome. She thought he could be Jack's brother—a younger, handsomer version of him.

He grinned at her. "How're you doing?"

She liked his voice, a light, pleasant baritone. A masculine voice, she reminded herself acidly. "Not too good," she said, looking into eyes that were slightly darker brown than Jack's. "I don't have any feel for roulette, I guess."

"It's just pure luck. Sometimes the numbers run for you, you know, like you suddenly start hitting jackpots for no reason." As Diana nodded, he continued, "But I've made money at it sometimes." He grinned again. "Honest I have. I know everybody says they win at gambling."

Diana smiled. She asked, testing his knowledge of the game, "What are the best percentage bets?"

"They all have about the same percentage," he replied, the correct answer. He explained the roulette layout—which she already knew well—indicating the odds and payoffs after each spin of the wheel, but she listened to him, quite willing to be distracted.

She had lost twenty dollars after a few more minutes of play, and she got up. "That's enough for me, but I've enjoyed the lesson."

"Wait a minute," he said, "sit down for just one second, okay? My name's Chick Benson." He looked at her for a moment, expectantly, "My real name's Charles but everybody calls me Chick. So did the newspapers. I met a girl one time who recognized my name. Football."

Diana sat down, looking at him carefully, and thinking. "Chick Benson," she repeated. "No, I'm afraid not."

"I was all-American nine years ago. At Kentucky."

"Really? What position?" she asked, thinking that he lacked the physical size, the bulk for football.

"Wide receiver."

"Oh. A glamor position. No wonder you don't look like Bubba Smith."

His pleasure was evident. "So you know a little about football."

"Just pro, not college."

"Most girls don't know anything at all. That's why I was surprised this one girl did."

"One thing I do know about the college game is that all-American players are the best in the country. You must be very proud of that."

"Thanks. Yeah. That's one thing they can't ever take away from me. This one girl who recognized my name, she remembered reading about me in the papers. What's your name?"

Diana hesitated. "Joyce Carol Oates," she said, thinking of the latest novel she had read. A bearded man on the other side of her chuckled.

"You go by all three names?"

"Call me Joyce," Diana said. The bearded man chuckled again.

"Would you like a drink? I'd enjoy buying you a drink."

She appraised him. He really did look a lot like Jack. And she had not thought about Lane Christianson for at least fifteen minutes. "Okay," she said.

She sat across from him in a cool, quiet area just off the casino. She had caught Vivian's eye as she walked with Chick Benson, and Vivian had nodded vigorously, beaming in approval. Diana had smothered a laugh, thinking how unimpressed Vivian would be with an all-American wide receiver from Kentucky. First Diana would have to explain what an all-American was, and then a wide receiver; and then Vivian would snort, "Another jock. Another little boy playing another silly game." Vivian's first husband had been a sports fanatic to the complete neglect of everything else—most grievously, Vivian.

As they sipped their drinks and watched the crowd circulate through the casino, she asked, "Why didn't you turn pro?"

"Oh I did," he said mournfully, and related a lengthy story of a second round draft by the Philadelphia Eagles, then details of torn ligaments at training camp, injured reserve lists, team physicals, waiver lists, tryouts with various other teams. With increasing bitterness he talked about broken promises and heavy-handed politics in the National Football League, the destruction of the opportunity he deserved after being all-American.

His was a dream irretrievably broken, and she listened sympathetically, asking questions, drawing his story from him, touched by the pain in his voice, on his face.

Eventually they went on to other subjects, making light conversation; she found him pleasant, engaging—not a mental giant, certainly, but attractive. She realized with increasing elation that she did find him attractive, and decided she didn't care if he had the intelligence of a gnat. She liked his body, his crisp masculine gestures and movements, his face, his voice. She did like men. Men were attractive to her. Perhaps she was recovering from this other aberration like getting over the flu. It had been just a temporary obsession—a schizophrenic and unreal Diana Holland who had been so weak with want in the presence of Lane Christianson.

"When do you go back to L.A.?" Chick Benson asked. He was also from Los Angeles, a steel salesman, living in the Marina.

"Thursday. You?"

"Tomorrow," he said regretfully. "I've had such a great time. Skiing is fantastic here. You really ought to try it."

"So I've been told."

"Why don't we go up to my room and have another drink?"

"Let's play blackjack for a while," she countered.

Finding a congenial dealer and cards that ran fairly well, they played blackjack for several hours, bantering and laughing. Diana won sixty dollars; Chick Benson, betting cautiously, won twenty.

"How about that drink?" he asked.

She glanced at her watch. "I'm meeting friends for dinner in a few minutes. Are you going to be around? I could call you. Say about eight?"

"Room fourteen-forty-nine. You mean it, Joyce?"

"As sure as my name's Joyce Carol Oates."

She had dinner with Vivian and John at the Summit, Harrah's rooftop restaurant. In a luxurious white leather booth in softly lit, romantic surroundings, she gazed at Lake Tahoe and the Sierras, watching a sunset that reduced even Vivian to silence. When she realized she was thinking of Lane and her reaction to this magnificence, she pushed the thoughts from her and concentrated on making conversation with Vivian and John. John's arm was around Vivian; Diana thought Vivian was suffering her presence. But she was suspicious that John was preening, playing the role of male peacock, a happy and contented female at his side, showing off his sexual prowess to an unattached female. Diana chided herself for her uncharitable thoughts; John was buying her dinner at a very expensive restaurant. He seemed to bring out a cynical, ungenerous side of her. Could she be jealous—subconsciously—that he was having sex with Vivian? She sipped wine, smiling with amusement. No, John was just a jerk, that was all.

Perhaps she should have brought Chick, to feel less an extra wheel. But Chick was not particularly interesting, and he and John would undoubtedly have talked sports — to Vivian's intense displeasure and boredom.

Diana continued to sip wine, staring out the window, part of her mind listening to Vivian's chatter. She considered whether she should meet Chick Benson. She would not go to his room, certainly, but they could have a drink, gamble together . . . She wasn't sure what she wanted, or needed, to do.

The sky darkened. Lights sparkled around the Lake as she finished dinner. The restaurant became intimately, darkly romantic. Diana's eyes were drawn and held by the figure of a woman making her way through the dining room, a woman wearing black, her movements graceful elegance, her body tall and slender, her hair blonde. The memory of Lane's face in her hands penetrated her; memories of Lane's hands and mouth filled her body with desire until she was hot and tremulous with it.

She picked up her wine glass. If it was sex she needed, she could do something about that.

She called Chick Benson from the lobby of the Sahara.

"Joyce? It's really you?"

"I told you I'd call," she said.

"I was betting you wouldn't."

"Why?"

"I just thought you wouldn't. Will you come up?"

He was drinking vodka with Seven-up. "That okay with you or should I call room service?"

"No, it's fine."

He mixed her drink and handed it to her and then took her into his arms, kissed her lightly. "Just to show you I'm a good guy," he said, releasing her.

She sipped her drink, wincing at the sweetness and the strong vodka content, and looked out the window at dark pines against the glowing mountains. "I thought you were a good guy before," she said.

"Good." He kissed her again, pushing his tongue into her mouth. She pulled away, annoyed.

"How about some music?" He switched off the television set and turned on the radio near the bed, adjusting the knobs. "That's better. You a feminist?"

She was startled by the question. "Why do you ask?"

"Just curious. I like to know how women feel about it."

"Well, I suppose I am. I'm for women's rights. Why?" she asked again, still puzzled by his question. "Are you?"

"Sure," he said, striding over to her, taking her into his arms again. She clasped his arms, her hands following the seams of his shirt over the breadth of his shoulders.

He kissed her, his tongue scouring inside her mouth, his hands roughly pressing her hips into him. Repelled, she broke away, and decided to leave.

He caught her in his arms again. "You're one of those soft pretty women," he told her. "I didn't think you were one of those feminists but you can never tell anymore. They come to my room—but they think they know better than I do how I should use my balls. I think most of them are really a bunch of lesbos."

He undressed her slowly, gentle with her. Hands on his shoulders, his chest, she tried to feel his hands and mouth with pleasure. He carried her to the bed and undressed himself.

His hands explored her body. "You're really lush. Pretty."

She moved under his mouth in a discomfort that was apparently interpreted as pleasure; he quickly pushed himself between her legs, rubbing against her without entering her.

"No," she gasped, horrified, struggling, beating her hands on his shoulders.

"You mean yes." He seized her hands and thrust into her, his mouth covering hers.

She jerked her mouth away and lay whimpering as he battered into her, his face against her neck, his hot breath burning her. As his movements abruptly quickened, she said desperately, swept by rising nausea, "I have no protection."

"You what," he gasped. "Jesus Christ, Christ you stupid—" His body shuddered and he wrenched himself out of her. A moment later his hot panting body collapsed across her.

He finally rolled off her. "Jesus," he said. "You could've told me, Joyce. Before. Why didn't you—what are you, Catholic?"

"Catholic," she whispered, her eyes closed, her stomach wet with him.

"We could've done something if you'd told me. Well, we made it anyway. Now you can tell your friends you made it with an all-American football player."

He was grinning when she opened her eyes. "I guess we need a shower, Joyce. Especially you. Unless you want to wear what I did on your stomach. How about a shower together?"

"No," she said. "Uh, why don't you go ahead? I need a few minutes to . . . collect myself. You know how women are."

"Oh. Sure."

She scrubbed herself quickly and savagely with a pillowcase, dressed swiftly, frantically as the shower ran; but he emerged, water dripping from him, his hips wrapped in a towel.

"I kind of thought you might think about leaving. I'll make it better for you. Look. Why don't we go down and gamble for a while? I'll get some rubbers. Stay overnight with me. I'll make it better for you, Joyce," he said, striding toward her as she walked to the door. "I'll make it so good. You'll love it. Stay with me," he pleaded.

She opened the door before she answered. "I think I'd rather become a feminist lesbo."

Something thudded against the door as she slammed it. She ran down the hall suddenly afraid that he would pursue her even wrapped in his towel. She wondered what he had thrown.

Urgently, she searched for Vivian and found her with John at a craps table in Harrah's. "I need to talk to you," she said in a low tone to Vivian. "Bad."

Vivian looked at her and without a word took her arm and led her to an empty section of slot machines.

"I need a favor, Viv. Desperately. Please let me have your room to take a bath."

Vivian stared at her. "You look sick, Diana. Are you sick?"

She managed a wan smile. "Is there such a thing as consenting rape?"

"Yeah, it's called marriage. What are you talking about, Diana?" Then she stared at Diana, stricken. "Oh my God did you—"

"Please, Viv—"

"Did you do this because of what I said? I'll kill myself."

"No. No. Not at all. But I'm going to die if I don't take a bath."

"Why don't I take you to the cabin?"

"No, Viv. I need to do this quickly. Now. *Please.*"

"All right. Sure. I'll tell John you feel dizzy in the altitude or something."

Vivian brought her up to the room and Diana said, "Go on back. Please. I need to be by myself. Could you give me an hour?"

"Sure. Sure, honey." Vivian hugged her warmly.

As soon as the door closed behind Vivian, Diana went into the bathroom and allowed herself to think about Chick Benson, leaning low over the sink as she threw up. She turned the taps fully on, and retched for some minutes after all her dinner had come up, her stomach continuing to convulse. She rinsed her mouth with mouthwash, and then rummaged through Vivian's cosmetic kit and suitcase. She found a disposable toothbrush which she used and discarded, and with conscienceless calm she assembled and used Vivian's douche bag. Then she ran bath water, filling the tub half full, and after lowering her body into it she ran hot water until the tub was almost full and her body felt parboiled. She scrubbed her skin till it burned.

She drained the tub and filled it half full again with lukewarm water. She lay back, and only then did she allow herself to think of Lane, Lane's arms around her, until her trembling and nausea stopped.

After she dressed, she sat in an armchair, the room in darkness, and watched the lights of traffic moving down Highway 50, thinking calmly, dispassionately.

Diana Holland, you have really made a mess of things. You let that crude animal do that to you, but you wouldn't let a tender sensitive woman—someone you care for—do what both of you want. Not performing an act—does that make your want of it not exist? If you had made love with her last night, would that have made you less a person? Less a woman? She is a beautiful, extraordinary person. You not only could do worse, you have done worse. When you let a drunk paw you for four years in the sanctified state of marriage, for instance. When you let a man defraud you for five years, for instance. Tonight, for instance.

What is it that you're afraid of, Diana Holland? What you feel? What other people think? Where is your courage? Your honesty? Your self-esteem? And furthermore, Diana Holland, what do you care how many men or women she's had? Did she care how many you've had? She wanted you. Just hope she still does.

She found Vivian, catching her eye to blow her a kiss. Crossing the parking lot to the car, she shoved her hands into her jacket pockets against the cold and felt a stiff piece of paper. She drew out a small card and walked under a floodlight to look at it. It was Lane's business card. She turned it over and saw neat printing on the back, a San Francisco address and phone number. She stood still, examining the card, the printing, turning it over and over in her fingers. There was a dot of ink below the phone number; Lane had started to write something and had changed her mind. There was nothing to write, Diana reflected. Giving her this card had said everything.

Feeling as if she had the gentle touch of Lane's fingers on her skin, she replaced the card in her pocket and went to her car.

It was just before ten when she arrived at the cabin. She saw Lane through the window, in dark pants and a blue velvet pullover, sitting on the hearth with her hands around her knees, her back against the stone of the fireplace. She was looking at the door, unable to see out the window because of the reflections. Diana knew she had heard the sound of the car.

"The way you talked I thought you'd be a lot later than this," Liz said as she walked in the door.

"I decided I'd rather be here," she said, and looked at Lane. Lane's eyes were blue against the blue of her pullover; they looked almost bruised.

"Are you still ahead?" Chris asked.

"Yes. I will be till I leave, if I don't do anything stupid."

"How do you do it?" Madge asked sourly.

"Luck," Diana answered.

"Well, I'm glad to see you," Liz said. "How about you and me head to head in Scrabble?"

"You're playing a game," Diana demurred. Liz, Madge, and Chris were gathered around the coffee table; Millie was strumming her guitar. "Besides, I want to take a shower." Her skin had begun to crawl as unwelcome memory crept into her mind.

"We're finished," Madge said, yawning. "Chris and I are going to bed. We're bushed."

"Lane and Chris just took showers," Liz said. "It'll take a half hour for the water to heat up again. How about it?"

Concern had risen in her. Lane had not spoken, or moved. Diana shrugged and said to Liz, "Okay."

"Would you like some wine?" Lane asked, getting up.

"We still have some?" she said with relief, and gratefully, thinking that a sip or two would be medicinal for her very empty stomach.

"Yes. We do."

As she accepted her wine glass from Lane, their eyes met. Her fingers touched Lane's. Lane's fingers released the glass slowly.

Liz laid out the Scrabble game. Lane returned to the fireplace, sitting again with her back against the stone, one leg drawn up, a hand dangling over her knee.

"I think I'll turn in, too," Millie said, and put her guitar in its case.

"I want to sit on this side of the table," Diana said to Liz. "So I can look at the fire."

She looked at Lane. Lane's lips curved into a faint smile.

Diana arranged and formed words with her tiles, looking up from time to time, knowing each time she would meet eyes made blue by the deep blue of Lane's pullover; and when she looked away she felt the blueness on her, warming her skin, her body, her blood.

Lane was standing by the window when Diana climbed the ladder. She remained there as Diana pulled up the ladder and lowered the trapdoor. "I didn't notice who won your game," she said.

"Neither did I," Diana said, coming to her.

Lane took her hands. "Diana," she said softly, "I'm so glad you came back. I didn't know . . . I would never have done anything to hurt you—"

"I know."

"I thought . . . I felt from your response last night . . . You're a very responsive woman. I thought what was happening between us was what you wanted, too."

"It was." Diana added with a small smile, "Women can be very difficult."

"Yes." Lane's teeth looked very white as she smiled. Her fingers entwined with Diana's. "Nothing will happen tonight that you don't want."

Diana looked directly into her eyes. "There is nothing," she said carefully, "that could happen tonight that I wouldn't want."

She was in Lane's arms, her body softening, yielding, seeking the tightness of her arms. Holding her closely, Lane said, her voice almost inaudible, "You never leave doubt that I'm holding a woman."

Diana whispered needfully, "Please, just hold me." Warmth was pervading her body, and a feeling of peace.

The window rattled in a strong gust of wind. The pines shook and moaned. Diana shivered and felt Lane's arms again tighten. Lane murmured, "Come to bed. You'll be in my arms all night."

The window rattled again; the cabin creaked in a sudden gust. Sitting on the side of the bed, Lane said, "The wind . . . so strong . . . I turned on the heater to keep us warm." Her voice was distracted; her hands were unfastening Diana's pajamas. "I want so much to look at you," she whispered.

Diana lay nude, warm and weak under her gaze. Lane said quietly, "I thought I had imagined how lovely you would be."

Diana lost awareness of her own nudity as she undressed Lane. Lane sat gracefully, patiently; Diana was slow with her, sliding the pajama top from her shoulders, contemplating her for long moments, absorbing the slender lines of her, the warm tones of her skin, the perfect round fullness and hang of her small breasts, the nipples firming even as Diana looked at them. She drew Lane's pajamas over her hips shyly, hesitantly, gazing at the small mound of pale delicate hair, the curving, firm, athletic lines of her thighs and legs. Diana lay back on the bed, mute, holding her hands.

"Do you want the light out?" Lane asked, bending over her.

"No."

"Neither do I. I can't look at you enough."

"You are so beautiful," whispered Diana, and reached for her.

Dimly, Diana heard Lane make an inarticulate sound. Lips touched Diana's ear, warm breath, a sighing: "Oh soft . . . warm silk."

Inside her arms, down her legs, on every surface of her body that pressed against the woman she held in her arms, Diana felt exquisite softness. Her senses were flooded and stunned with softness. Strangely disoriented, she said, "Lane," to hear her own voice.

Lane cradled Diana's head in her hands and looked into her eyes. She said gently, "Are you all right?"

Diana's hands touched, moved over her bare slender shoulders.

She looked into eyes that were a deep gray-blue in the shadows and dim light from the lamp. She thought: What I feel is your body. The realization penetrated her, and a powerful stirring of desire.

"Yes," she whispered, and blonde hair was silk in her hands, flowing, sifting through her fingers as she drew Lane's mouth down to hers.

They kissed deeply, slowly, again and again, caressing each other, Diana's hands exploring the softness of Lane with gentle wonder. Inhaling the fragrance of her, Diana kissed her throat, her shoulders; but Lane took her mouth away to bring Diana's lips again to hers. Lane's hands were warm and slow on her, and she kissed her body lingeringly, without pattern, her mouth a sweet melting where it touched, and Diana heard her muffled whisper, "Dear God . . . so wonderful . . ." Gentle hands caressed her breasts as Lane kissed them, long slow kisses, sweetest stroking of her nipples, and Diana succumbed to pleasure, sighing, stirring, murmuring in her pleasure.

Lane's hands came to her body again, and overwhelmed her. She was ardent in Lane's hands; she moved and turned and arched under the hands feeling, caressing, exciting her, and she heard gasps of excitement in Lane's light, rapid breathing. No longer gentle, Lane held Diana tightly to her, pressing the softness of her body into her, kissing her in an intensity of desire. Drawing breath deeply into her, her body vibrant with sensation, Diana gasped her desire as Lane's hand came again to her thighs.

"Diana . . . Oh God," breathed Lane against her mouth. Her hand had cupped, fingers gently, wetly caressing. Electrified with pleasure, Diana arched and trembled, all her breath held within her. Lane's fingers stilled, and in a moment her hair fell over Diana's legs. Diana gasped, arched again as Lane kissed inside her thighs. Lane moaned, a low rapturous sound; and then her mouth was paralyzing softness, paralyzing pleasure, and Diana was dissolved into ecstasy, her body taut and trembling, opening to it slowly, fully, perfectly, like a flower; filling with ecstasy, becoming ecstasy to her core; ecstasy finally so vivid that her body stilled and powerfully gathered. Her hips rose to thrust once; and she became incandescent with orgasm.

She lay in Lane's arms struggling for breath, her body hammered by heartbeats.

Her face in Diana's hair, Lane whispered "Diana," murmuring it over and over.

Remembering the women below, Diana swallowed and found her voice, asking through labored breaths, "Did I make too much . . . Could . . . anybody hear?"

"No," Lane answered, her voice husky. "Only me."

Her body tranquil, pervaded by exquisite lassitude, she sat beside Lane, eyes closed, seeing with her mind the beauty of the body she caressed, the warm sculpture under her hands. She lingered for long moments over the extraordinary richness of breasts that were pliant under her fingers, yet so easily resumed their shape of sensual symmetry; and over soft fine hair, touching not to arouse, but to absorb texture. Her hands moved slowly down over her legs, holding the calves for a moment, then the ankles and feet.

She thought: Now I have the beauty of you in me to keep forever.

She laid the length of her body against Lane, and looked into gray-blue eyes that held an expression she finally decided was questioning. She said, "You know how very beautiful you are."

"Only if you tell me. I need to know it from you. From you."

Moved by the defenselessness of the words, swept by tenderness, Diana said, "I hope I can show you."

With increasing excitement and intense enjoyment, she caressed Lane sensuously with her hands, kissing her breasts and the delicate hollows of her body with light tasting strokes of her tongue, acute to responses very different from her own: Lane's body quiescent, her pleasure evident in her breathing, her hands in Diana's hair holding Diana's mouth to her. She brushed her hair over Lane, and then her breasts, pressing, then undulating them into her as she heard the pleasure she gave. "Beautiful, you're so beautiful," she whispered. "Everywhere I touch you is beautiful." She kissed down curving softness to the top of her legs, her fingers gently, shyly touching the soft pale hair next to her cheek. She heard Lane's faint whisper, "I need to hold you."

Diana came to her and took her into her arms. Lane brought Diana's hand to her, closing her legs; and making soft sounds she slid her arms around her, hands clasping Diana's shoulders, face against her throat. Moved to tenderness, Diana explored the yielding softness, the delicateness of her, the warm wetness enveloping her fingers.

Lane's whisper was barely audible: "Could you . . . be inside me?"

"Anything," Diana whispered. "Like satin to me," she murmured, her fingers exquisitely enclosed, feeling tremors in Lane's body. She moved her fingers, caressing very lightly with her hand.

"Yes. Oh . . ."

Lane's hands slowly tightened on her shoulders, her body tense and trembling, hips in erratic then urgent rhythm, her breathing quickening to ragged gasps. Then she became still, rigid; she made tiny sounds against Diana's throat; her fingers dug convulsively into Diana's shoulders; and Diana felt a quivering, felt the delicate body of the woman clinging so tightly to her begin to shudder, like leaves in the wind.

Diana's heart thudded painfully as she held Lane, now quietly breathing, in her arms. Lane moved languorously, contentedly against her, blonde hair spilling over Diana's breasts. She had pressed her body into Diana even as she had quivered against her fingers, and then had closed her legs to hold Diana inside her; it had been some time before she had allowed Diana to take her fingers from her.

Longing to touch her, caress her again, Diana said, "I want to kiss your back. Would you like that?"

"Mmm," Lane murmured, smiling, kissing Diana's breasts before she turned over.

Diana explored the planes and smooth graceful curves of her back, her hands lingering, sweeping lightly back and forth with sensual enjoyment in the deep curve between her back and the swell of her hips. She kissed her lightly, with puffs of warm air and strokes with the tip of her tongue, smiling as Lane made exaggerated purring sounds. She slipped her hands under her and cupped and caressed the softness of Lane's breasts, sighing, blissful in her enjoyment, and pressed her own breasts into her. Her mouth traveled slowly, and when her tongue began to brush the fine hair in the hollow at the base of her spine, Lane's nipples were swollen hard in her fingers.

In growing excitement, willing Lane not to roll over and stop her, Diana continued to descend her, feeling the plushness of cool hips pleasurably against her warm face, her tongue caressing in slow circles in the delicate crevice between her hips. Lane's breathing changed, deepened, and her hips became an undulation of pleasure. Her heart pounding, Diana moved a hand down into soft fine hair, fingers very gently seeking. Lane's breathing again became sharp intakes, and the motion of her hips changed, responding only to Diana's fingers. Diana said, "Turn over."

Suffused with pleasure and excitement, fully absorbed in her own sensation, she touched her lips to the soft fine hair, tasting the essence she had known with her fingers.

"God in heaven . . . Diana . . ."

Enthralled by the subtly changing, unique taste of her, she slowly discovered Lane with her mouth, her own excitement mounting with the growing fierceness of Lane's movements. Lane's hands in her hair guided her, finally becoming transfixed. She felt Lane's strong shudders in a powerful surging ecstasy of her own.

Thighs that had writhed in Diana's hands were now limp and seemed to have a poignant vulnerability as they fluttered and shivered. Lane's hands stirred weakly in Diana's hair; her breathing was deep and labored. Wanting only to hold her close, Diana tenderly drew her mouth from her, from the complex, lovely taste of her, the scent of her, like the sea.

They lay side by side, Lane holding Diana's hand, looking at it, pensively tracing a finger over her palm. She had been in Diana's arms for a long time, quiet and unmoving. She said, with a sideways glance at her, her voice soft and warm, "Are you planning any more ambushes?"

"Maybe, maybe not," Diana said, smiling.

"I remember the last time you said that. I asked if you were sure you were going to catch me during the encounter games."

"The first time I had my arms around you."

"You enjoyed it so much you dropped me," Lane teased.

"You deserved it. You didn't trust me."

Lane said seriously, "You're very trusting. You're a very courageous and honest person."

"Not so courageous," murmured Diana. "I don't know why you say that. You're very honest."

"With you, yes."

"Haven't you been honest with other women?"

Lane looked at her with a slow, deeply amused smile. "How many other women do you think there've been?"

"Thousands."

Lane laughed. "Why do you think so?"

"The way you know how to touch me."

Lane rolled over onto her stomach and propped herself on her elbows to smile down at Diana. "Have you already forgotten what you just did with me?"

Diana said awkwardly, "That just . . . happened."

"Yes. But how did you know how to touch me?"

"I . . . just knew. You made it very easy for me to know. From how you were with me, and . . . from myself, and there were things I thought you would like . . . and things I wanted to do."

"There were things I wanted to do, too. I wanted to please you, and I wanted to . . . do everything I did. And that's how I knew how to touch you."

Lane lay on her back again and locked her hands behind her head. She stared out the window. "When I was seventeen, Diana, there was someone. She was a year ahead of me in high school, a senior. We became friends. Friends," she repeated ironically. "I thought my friendship with her was some kind of gift from the gods. I'd never felt that close to anyone before except my father. We touched, often, and we held hands when we were alone. I justified that so easily, you know—we were unusually close friends and no one would understand how special our friendship was. What a fool, what an idiot I was. One night I was over at her house and we were in her bedroom watching television, holding hands, sitting on her bed. Her parents were out. We did that before, many times, but this time she put an arm around me and suddenly we were in each other's arms, and when we kissed I knew how much I'd wanted to all along. We took each other's clothes off. Her name was Carol. I was stunned by my sexual feeling, absolutely staggered by how her body felt to me. None of the boys I'd been with, and I wasn't a virgin then either, none of them had made me feel even remotely like that. Nothing happened between us—I was too terrified. I put on my clothes and fled. I wouldn't see her again. She finally gave up trying. I knew how badly I was hurting her, but I knew if I saw her again it would happen again, and I knew I wouldn't be able to stop it again."

"That was the only time?"

"Yes. I was so relieved when I fell in love with Mark, that I wanted him. And there've been men since him, of course, lots of them — God knows how many."

"Lane, your experience seems just part of adolescence. Didn't loving Mark prove that?"

"Seventeen is a little old for that kind of experience. You sound like some of my own rationalizations," she said with a little smile. "There wasn't a rationalization I didn't think of to explain my feeling for Carol. But I couldn't do anything about a woman whose face I can never see — she's come to me again and again in my dreams, for years."

"I think that's not an uncommon fantasy for women."

"Another of my rationalizations. I've never dared have a friendship like you have with Vivian. Just casual, superficial relationships with women like Madge. I would never take a chance after Carol that feeling or friendship with another woman might develop into physical attraction. From the beginning I felt very drawn to you. I didn't go gambling when you asked me because you were already too attractive to me."

"You still let me happen to you."

Lane said simply, "I seem to have no defense for you."

Diana said slowly, "I was the first for you."

"Yes. And more wonderful than any dream could ever be."

Diana was silent, remembering her, in context with this new knowledge. She said finally, "Lane, why didn't you tell me before? Last night? This morning?"

"I had no right to do anything. I've had the same fear of this as you, I've run from it for years. You had to make your own decision about it. It looked like it would turn out to be poetic justice, too. You running from me like I ran from Carol."

"What happened to her?"

"She lives in San Francisco. With another woman, I understand."

"How very lonely you've been."

"I work very hard. There've been men." She paused. "It wasn't so bad when Father was alive. We were so close. He got me through Mark's death. I almost didn't get through his. For a long terrible time I didn't want to live. My work saved me more than anything else."

"I wish I could have known you then."

"I don't know if I could have allowed it, Diana. If this could have

happened without circumstances like these." She continued
thoughtfully, "I thought you'd been with women before, the first
night. It seemed to me you made the first move, wanted us to kiss.
You were so hurt by the encounter games all I tried to do was hold
you, try to make everything all right—"

"Yes, and you were so gentle . . . it seemed right to kiss you. And
then all that day I wondered what you must think. And then last
night when you came to me like you did, I thought you were the one
with experience."

"What a strange time it's been for us. After our first night I was
too stunned to do anything but try and sort out my own feelings.
Then I realized you were upset, probably very worried. I tried to tell
you when we had the drink together. After that, I didn't have a
chance again."

"I thought you were telling me you didn't think anything of it,
that it wasn't important at all to you."

"Oh. That explains it. I waited for you in front of the window, I
thought we'd talk then. And you just went to bed. I couldn't figure
you out at all." She smiled. "I decided I just didn't get my message
across earlier and so I came to you."

"I was totally surprised. It was the last thing I expected."

"I should have realized. But I didn't understand until . . ." Lane
continued very softly, "There was nothing I could say or do. What a
terrible, ghastly feeling. All I could do was hope you wouldn't go back
to Los Angeles, and that would be the end. Did you find my card?"

"Yes. I was very glad to find it when I did."

"I should never have done that. But I just had to."

"I was afraid all the way driving back you'd decided you could
have a lot less trouble with any of those wiling women in San
Francisco."

Lane smiled. "I've had a terrible time over you. A menace on
skis. Falling down, almost running into trees. All I could think about
was you, how it feels to hold you and kiss you. You . . . you've never
felt an attraction to a woman before?"

"I . . ." She did not know how to describe her emotion for
Barbara, and she said, "A physical relationship . . . just never
occurred to me." She looked at Lane and said with simple honesty, "I
can't look at you without wanting you."

Lane moved to her. "And I want you. So very much."

Lane's mouth left hers to come to her body, and moved very slowly down her. She kissed lingeringly inside her thighs, fingers stroking intimately, gently. Trembling everywhere, Diana finally moaned. Then a much more exquisite stroking began.

Afterward, Lane lay with her head on Diana's stomach, holding Diana's hands tightly. "Sweet," she whispered. "Dear God, you taste so sweet."

Diana lay breathing rapidly; orgasm had been so strong she was still stunned by the power of it. Lane's breasts were between her legs and Lane pressed them into her, and then rubbed each taut nipple in her wetness, sighing, murmuring in her own pleasure as she flooded Diana again with sensation. When Diana's legs trembled, Lane's mouth came to her again, slow, more knowledgeable. Orgasm was yet stronger, her body utterly rigid and transfused with radiance.

Lane came to her and laid her body on her, fitting it to her, moaning when Diana wrapped her arms, her legs around her. Lane moved on her in a sensuous, prolonged caress, eyes closed. Diana's senses were engulfed, overwhelmed. Lane held Diana's face tightly in her hands and said in a ragged voice, her face hard, austere with desire, "I'm going to do this to you," and kissed her mouth with thrusts and strokes of her tongue, holding the turbulence of Diana's body under her with surprising strength. She brought her mouth to Diana's legs, and Diana's hips writhed and thrust uncontrollably, cries torn from her throat, until she was transfixed with orgasm, her body molten, feeling that even her bones were melting.

She lay in Lane's arms trembling and tearful. "I'm not crying," she said unsteadily.

"I know." Lane was kissing tears away as they formed at the corners of her eyes.

"It's more . . . each time."

"Yes. I know."

"I'm going to die from you."

"No you're not," Lane said seriously, matter-of-factly. She asked, "Do you want to sleep for a while?"

Diana moved her hands over her shoulders, then down the planes of her back to clasp the rich flesh of her hips. "No," she said. She turned to put Lane under her. "God no," she said, her mouth coming to Lane's breasts.

Outside the cabin, the wind howled and blew, shaking the

window with fierce gusts. The electric heater in their room whirred and ticked with heat.

Their bed became a chaos. The blanket fell onto the floor, pillows were everywhere, some on the floor; and Lane in orgasm pulled the sheets from their mooring. Diana's pleasure in Lane's body remained an unchanging intensity, and intermittently, there was her own luminous, consuming ecstasy.

Entwined, kissing, they heard women's voices faintly from below. Diana turned her face away. "You can't leave today." She extricated herself from Lane, sat up. "You just can't."

"No, I can't. I'll call from town."

Exultant, Diana asked, not really caring, "Is it a big problem?"

"I need to figure out how to take care of a few things. But the real problem is them." Lane gestured below. "Explaining why I'm staying another day."

"To go gambling with me. I talked you into it."

Lane nodded and sat up. "That might work. Madge'll think it's highly uncharacteristic, which it is. I'm very disciplined about my work. And Liz doesn't miss a thing. It's a good thing she had her back to me last night, couldn't see us look at each other."

Diana got out of bed and searched for their pajamas. "What would they suspect? Neither one of us has much of a history of this."

Lane smiled. "True. We were supposed to go skiing this morning and then I was supposed to leave this afternoon. If I leave tomorrow morning that'll put me in San Francisco . . ." She trailed off, thinking.

Diana heard the words San Francisco with a feeling of desolation.

"I think it'll look better if I ski for a couple of hours," Lane mused. "Come back here and change and meet you in town."

"I'll wait for you here," Diana said firmly.

"Skiing. I've got to go skiing. Oh cruel and unusual punishment. The last thing my body needs. Oh God." She collapsed across the bed.

Diana laughed at the sight of her sprawled in despair amid the tumble of their bed. "I've never seen anyone look less like a lawyer."

Lane pulled a sheet up over her, covering her face. Her voice through the sheet was muffled. "Dignity is so difficult when a person isn't wearing any clothes." She tossed the sheet aside and rubbed her eyes. "I need to think about what I've got scheduled tomorrow, how to take care of it. Why don't you go down? I'll straighten our room and get my thoughts together. God, look at this," she said, sitting up and surveying the bed.

Diana said impishly, "We were . . . enthusiastic."

Lane laughed. "Why don't you come back here for a minute before you put any clothes on?"

Some minutes later, her arms released Diana. "Good morning," she said, smiling into her eyes. "Do you feel as marvelous as I do?"

"Good morning," whispered Diana, smiling. "Yes."

She climbed down the ladder and waved to the group at the fire, and went into the bathroom. She splashed water on her face and stopped, suddenly weak from the scent of Lane on her fingers. She looked into the mirror and contemplated the radiance of her face, the utter fulfillment of her body. She wondered if she had given a similar gratification to Lane. Remembering that they had slept only a few hours the past three nights — Lane probably less — she decided that she would make Lane sleep that night, hold her soft, delicate body in her arms while she slept.

Smiling with the thought, she began to brush her hair. Startled, she leaned closer to the mirror and saw the pale blue of emerging bruises on her shoulders. It was crazy, she thought. Ravaged by an all-American Attila the Hun — and the gentlest person in the world leaves bruises.

She dressed and joined the group while Lane was in the bathroom. "I talked Lane into staying another day," she said. "Is that okay with you, Liz?"

"You did what?" Madge said.

"Sure, fine," Liz said. "She was the one who decided she had to get back early."

"I don't believe it," Madge said. "We had tickets to a play she'd been waiting months to see and she canceled at the last minute, some problem at work again. That's not the only time, either. She's a fanatic about her work."

"I used my powers of persuasion," Diana said, smiling. "I made her break out of her script."

The women laughed, but Madge said, "I know she's got problems at her office, that's why she was cutting this vacation short. What did you say to her?"

"Ask Lane," Diana said in exasperation as Lane joined them. Lane was a lawyer—she could use her verbal skill to fend off this pest of a woman.

Madge said with pointed sarcasm, "Lane, how did Diana manage to break through that wall of dedication?"

Lane said with a brilliant smile, "She convinced me that a touch of unpredictability will be good for my professional image."

"Can't hurt," Liz said indifferently.

Madge raised her eyebrows and sipped her coffee, contemplating Lane.

Chris said, "The other night Lane said you can make decisions about your life anytime, right up to the point of senility. Isn't that right, Lane?"

"That's right, Chris."

Madge nodded, evidently satisfied. "It's about time you showed a sign of being human."

Lane said with a sparkling glance at Diana, "I've got my weaknesses."

"Yeah? Name one," Liz challenged, grinning.

"Your food, Liz."

Liz beamed. "Let's have breakfast."

"I think it's wonderful you're staying," Chris said. "This little vacation is doing you a world of good. You and Diana look just glowing this morning."

Diana and Lane disposed of a huge quantity of eggs, ham, and pancakes. "It's this great mountain air and your great food, Liz," Diana murmured, looking at Lane. Lane's eyes glinted in amusement.

"Can I expect you both back for dinner?" Liz asked.

"No," Diana answered immediately, and then glanced at Lane.

Lane nodded, and smiled at Liz. "I plan to become a degenerate gambler."

Diana watched Lane walk swiftly down the road to her car, breath forming clouds in the cold. She warmed the car, a small silver

Mercedes, gunning the engine in the cold thin altitude for some time before driving off toward town.

The women left, except for Chris, who had decided at the last moment to take the day off from skiing. Disappointed, wanting to be alone to luxuriate in her thoughts, Diana sat beside the fire with a book in her hands, forcing sporadic conversation with Chris, drugged with the pleasure of memory, blissful in her waiting for Lane.

Lane returned soon after eleven o'clock, her skin color heightened, her pants patched with damp.

"How did you get so wet?" Chris asked, looking at her in concern.

"I wasn't Margot Fonteyn out there," Lane muttered, staring at her. "I'll be down in a few minutes," she added to Diana.

"I need to go upstairs too," Diana said.

As they stepped into their room Lane said in a low, vehement tone, "Why does she have to be here? I came back as soon as I could . . . I can't even hold you, I'm so wet and cold."

Diana sighed. "It's maybe just as well. Lane, would you wear that white silk blouse that ties at the throat?"

"Anything you want. As long as we're making requests, would you change into that white V-neck sweater?"

Diana pulled off her gold sweater and took the white cashmere from the drawer. Feeling Lane's eyes on her, she turned to her. Lane had stripped off her ski clothes and stood by the closet, her eyes fixed on Diana's breasts. Diana stared at her, eyes dropping to the wisp of white lace on her hips.

"My hands are warm now," Lane said.

"Lane, she might take it into her head to climb the ladder," Diana said with difficulty, a burning sensation within her, her nipples taut.

"I hate her."

"So do I."

Lane said, "Let's take my car. It's all warmed up."

"I like your car," Diana said.

"It was my father's. Would you like to drive it?"

"Not in all this ice and snow."

"Don't worry." Lane tossed her the keys. "I trust you."

Diana drove carefully, watching for slippery spots. The road was clear and dry, and she relaxed and enjoyed the car. "You've already been over this road," she accused, "you knew it was clear. I still don't know for sure if you trust me."

"I trust you."

Conscious of Lane looking at her she said, "This is a nice car for two people."

"Yes. Very intimate."

"It's hard for me to drive when you're looking at me."

"I'm only looking."

"Your looking is like touching."

Obediently looking out the windshield, Lane asked, "What did you do this morning?"

"Remembered." Diana asked, "Why did you get so wet and cold? Was the snow bad?"

"No, I just fell a lot. And I sat in a snowbank for a long time and remembered, too. I think that's when I got my clothes so wet."

"I don't like the idea of you falling. You could hurt yourself."

"I won't."

Diana parked at Harrah's. "I know it's too early for a drink," she said as they walked across the parking lot, "but Harrah's has a place with a beautiful view. It would be nice to be alone with you that way."

"Okay. Good."

"I need to find Viv, explain why I won't be playing with her today. Leave it to me, I know how to take care of it."

"We're two strangers in a strange town," Lane observed. "How can so many people be cluttering up the landscape?"

They found Vivian at Harvey's. "I saw you earlier this morning, dear," Vivian said to Lane. "At Harrah's, over by the jewelry counter. I said hello and you looked right through me."

"I did? Oh God I'm sorry." Lane looked so embarrassed that Diana and Vivian laughed. "I had phone calls to make and there was a lot on my mind."

Vivian shrugged. "I figured something was going on. Don't worry, Vivian's ego is indestructible." She smiled at Lane. "Just like her curiosity." As Lane did not answer, she shrugged again.

Diana looked at Vivian, puzzled, then dismissed her feeling. She said, "I'm going to teach Lane blackjack, then I thought we'd drive over to the North Shore. Want to come along?"

"Lord no. It's dead as a doornail over there at the best of times. Enjoy yourselves, girls. Vivian will stay where there's a few warm bodies and play her slot machines."

As they rode up on the elevator Lane said, "I assume you knew she'd turn you down."

Diana nodded. "I think we're reasonably free of people for a while."

A few minutes later they sat gazing at a panorama of trees and snow. Lane said, "What a wonderful place."

The waiter brought their wine. Lane had been looking at her intently, and when he left she said, "Your eyes are a very light brown, but they have a few flecks of green in them in the daylight."

"My mother's eyes were green."

"You've never mentioned your mother, just your father."

"She died when I was four. Hit and run, right in front of our house. They never caught anybody."

"What a tragedy," murmured Lane. "Do you remember her at all?"

"Just vaguely. After that there was a procession of women through the house, all of them trying to mother me — I think to impress Dad. But he never remarried. What about your mother?"

"She's married, she lives in Pacifica. We're a little closer since Father died, but still not close. She divorced Father when I was ten, and I fought to be with him, I worshipped him so. That's hard for any mother to understand or forgive, I guess. I have Father's hair and eyes, and I was definitely his daughter. She had every reason to divorce him, though. He was a womanizer. A very good-looking man — and there were a great many women."

"What did you think about that?"

"At the time I was jealous, I didn't realize how meaningless all those women were. I've been thinking about it again the past few days, Diana, and about Madge's scripts. He had a lot of women — I've had a lot of men. I remember before Carol happened, I remember so clearly . . ." Lane's face was somber. "He told me women with other women was the most irrational, the most contemptible, the most laughable of all the perversions."

Diana said, astonished, "Why would he say that? How could he possibly know? How can any man know that?"

"I don't think he did know. I think maybe he . . . sensed something in me."

"It's possible . . . and now I understand why you ran from what you needed. It wasn't a matter of personal courage—it was your fear of being condemned by the person whose opinion was more powerful than anyone else's."

Lane said slowly, "There's something to be said for Madge's scripts. Yet I know Father didn't want me to have the same kind of life he had. I see now that he was essentially lonely, trapped by his energies, and he didn't want that for me. Mark wasn't what he had in mind for me to marry—Mark's goals were too modest. But he grew very fond of him, and I'd run so wild before—he wanted to see me married, happy with one man. When Mark died I think Father was almost as broken by it as I was."

"Will you tell me about Mark?"

"Yes, if you like. He was a commercial artist. Good-looking—to me, anyway. Very slim, dark brown hair not quite to his shoulders, dark brown eyes. Sensitive features, he was a sensitive man, very unusual. He simply ignored all my little games."

"Games?"

"Domination games. The you-better-compromise-because-I-won't kind of games. They're games I always seem to play, and always win. Except winning is losing, of course. My male relationships have been played out on a battlefield. I'm not proud of that, Diana, it's just how it is. Except for Mark."

"Why was he different?" She felt a compelling need to learn about this man Lane had loved.

"I think . . . he just refused to get his ego involved. And he truly cared for me. He'd say, 'You're acting like a child again, Lane,' and go out and work in his garden. He had a small house with a rock garden with all kinds of delicate ferns and unusual plants. He liked to do solitary things like that. Sometimes he'd just walk. For miles, and come back and tell me droll stories of things he'd seen. He had a unique view of things I can't really describe. He liked to cook. He liked waiting on me, I think it was another kind of caring for me. He was like a brother, a friend to me in many ways."

"I'm glad you happened to him."

"That's a nice thing to say. But I'm glad he happened to me. He opened things in me. I was too young to really know it then and probably didn't show it much. I guess I haven't to anyone, till you."

Lane said, forming her words tentatively, "I don't understand about your friend who hurt you."

"I'm still trying to understand it myself. I didn't marry Jack—my one marriage was like being in jail. But maybe it was one of the things that caused him to place less value on our relationship." She said the words easily that she had not said to anyone: "There were other women. He swears it will never happen again, he wants another chance, but I can't find it in me to forgive him."

Lane's eyebrows rose slightly. "He must be insane. You're the kind of desirable, responsive woman men dream of."

Diana said awkwardly, "I'm . . . different with you . . . than I've ever been with anybody."

"I'm different with you, too."

"I have nothing to compare you with."

"Nor me with you."

Diana said, "Do you know how much your eyes change color? Right now they're exactly between gray and blue. That's what they are most often. Beautiful."

"Thank you. Diana . . . I saw bruises on your shoulders this morning." She sighed. "I don't remember doing it. I can't believe I could do that to you."

They were leaning toward each other, talking softly. Diana said, "You had your arms around me, your hands on my shoulders. Your fingers kept tightening."

"I'm sorry."

Looking into her eyes, wishing she could take her hands, Diana said, "I mean this, don't be sorry at all. You were so gentle with me . . . It was during the first time for you and your hands helped me to know . . . how you wanted me to . . . touch you."

"I remember. I remember holding your shoulders. I didn't know I was pressing hard with my fingers."

"You weren't, until suddenly." Diana touched fingertips to her sweater, to the bruises. "I like having them."

"Did I hurt you other times . . . when I wasn't aware?"

"The second time your hands were in my hair. And one other

time. The other times your hands were gripping the blanket or the sheet."

"You don't clench your hands at all." Lane held out her hands, slim fingers fully extended and as far apart as she could stretch them. "Your hands look like this. Completely rigid. And trembling, like the rest of you."

Diana did not reply, not trusting her voice. Toying with her wine glass, Lane looked out the window. Diana watched her fingers stroke frost from the glass.

After a time Diana asked, "What are you thinking about?"

Lane brought her gaze back to Diana. The planes of her face seemed hardened, almost ascetic, and her eyes were perceptibly deeper in color, almost gray. "How you taste," she said. "Did you really need to ask?"

Diana looked away, out the window, her mind swept clean of thought, her heart thudding dully. Lane said, "Why don't we talk about blackjack and what I should know to play it?"

Diana began a discussion of the game, grateful for the distraction, and Lane listened attentively, asking questions.

"Sometimes everybody's friendly, including the dealer," Diana concluded, "but it's usually a quiet game, and usually sexless. The men pay very little attention to you."

"That will be a refreshing change."

"Does how you look bother you?"

"Sometimes."

"Would you prefer to be less attractive than you are?"

"Not at the moment," Lane said, placing a bill on the check. "Don't argue about who pays, okay?"

Diana gazed at her.

Lane looked away and said, her voice husky, "I suppose we should be . . . a little careful how we look at each other."

"Lane . . . when you go back to San Francisco—"

"I don't want to talk about that," Lane said evenly. "I don't want to think about anything but you and being with you today and tonight."

They went into the casino.

* * * * *

"For luck," Diana said. She had placed ten dollars in the betting square in front of Lane.

The dealer drew a blackjack, to groans around the table.

"That wasn't nice," Lane observed, taking a fifty-dollar bill from her wallet.

"That's right, honey," said the dealer, a husky woman with tightly curled black hair. "I've been known to be downright nasty."

Diana, chuckling, looked at her nameplate. She asked, puzzled, "Your name is Benny?"

"Nope. Carlotta. Lost my nametag. Found this one in back."

The table of players laughed. The dealer shrugged. "It's a rule we wear a nametag. Who cares what it says? What do you think, what's Benny short for?"

"How about Bernadette?" Lane suggested.

"Bernadette, Benny," the dealer said, changing Lane's fifty dollars into chips. "I guess so. Isn't that the name of one of those saints who died saving her virginity?"

"I think so," Lane said.

"Would that be dumb enough?"

Lane leaned over and placed ten dollars in the square in front of Diana, her arm brushing hers; the scent of her perfume reached Diana. "For luck," she said.

Their eyes met. Diana looked down, at Lane's waist, at the curving of her body encircled by the small gold links of her belt; her eyes followed the line of her thigh. Desire washed through her, a huge warm wave.

She watched Lane's cards, leaning close to her, explaining, enjoying her reactions to her wins and losses, looking at her as she played, at her hands handling cards and money, her long slender fingers, the slightly squared-off nails.

The man on the other side of Lane asked something Diana did not hear. "No, I'm taken," Lane answered abstractedly, with the barest glance at him, and picked up her cards, ignoring him.

She looked at the delicate bones of Lane's wrists, remembering how she had kissed them and traced them with her tongue. She saw the outline of Lane's breasts through her blouse, and that her nipples were hardened. The dealer was tapping in front of her, waiting. "I'm sorry," Diana said, and looked at her cards.

She said to Lane, "You have pretty hands."

"Thank you," Lane said in an amused voice, "I'm so glad you like them." She moved restlessly in her chair.

Diana thought of the slender body under the white silk shuddering in her arms, and another wave of desire swept powerfully through her, closing up her throat.

The dealer was tapping in front of her again. "You seemed all right before, dear. Was it something I said that put you to sleep?"

"Let's do something else." Lane picked up her money.

"I'm having trouble concentrating," Diana said to the dealer, "I'm sorry."

"It's all right, babe. Lots of people up here don't get enough sleep."

"What do you want to do?" Lane asked as they walked through the casino.

Diana shrugged, sighed. "My second choice would be to go for a drive, I guess."

"What's your first choice?"

Diana said with a faint smile, "Did you really have to ask?"

"Yes." Lane took her arm, led her to a deserted section of tables, and looked at her intently. "Tell me. Tell me what you really want to do, Diana."

"I want to go to bed with you. And you know it."

"I want that too. Right now. What about a motel?"

"Yes."

"I'll drive. You look."

Lane pulled out of Harrah's parking lot. "Right at the next corner, at Stateline," Diana instructed. "Why did it take so long to think of this?"

"Because we're both used to having this initiative taken for us. I've never even been physically aggressive before two nights ago. At least we learn fast. Maybe we can find a place in the pines."

Diana watched Lane as she drove—the slim leather-booted foot on the accelerator pedal, free leg arched to rest gracefully against her thigh. Her gaze traveled up to gloved hands on the steering wheel, and then to Lane's face, edged with gold, her profile clear and lovely against the bright sky.

Lane teased, "It's hard for me to drive when you're looking at me."

"I'm only looking," Diana said, smiling.

"You're right, looking can be like touching." Lane glanced over at her. "Besides, you're supposed to be watching for a place."

Diana hung up their coats, and Lane opened the drapes to lighten their room. "God, look at that," Lane said, gesturing to the Lake and the encircling chalk-white mountains.

"Yes," Diana said, her gaze on Lane, coming up from behind and sliding her arms around her, bathing her face in perfumed hair. She kissed the back of her neck and felt tremors in Lane's body. Lane's hands held Diana's arms to her, and she tilted her head back so their faces touched. Diana's fingers opened Lane's belt; she pulled it slowly through the belt loops until the small gold links lay in her palm. She released Lane and turned her and took the thin cord of the white silk blouse in her hands—and saw the rapid pulse beat in her throat. She took her into her arms; but Lane was lethargic, almost inert, breathing shallowly. Diana looked at her, saw that her face was hardened into the same tense ascetic beauty she had seen in the bar at Harrah's. Her eyes had deepened to gray and looked blurred, unfocused.

Lane said dully, "I seem to be . . . in a very bad way about you."

"It's all right. It's all right."

Lane stood passively as Diana undressed her gently and without pause. "I don't want to . . . be like this."

"It's all right. Believe me." Diana's voice was strained with the effort to convey conviction. "Believe me it's all right." She pulled off her own clothes and led Lane to the bed.

"I need to hold you," Lane said helplessly.

Diana sat on the bed, drew Lane down, astride her.

"Oh God, Diana," Lane whispered, her arms tight around Diana's shoulders.

"Lane," she answered, fingers seeking her.

Lane's body crumpled, her breath leaving her. Diana caressed, glided in her, but Lane's body arched, her hips thrust in their own urgent rhythm, her arms trembling around Diana's shoulders, her breath ragged and gasping. "Lane," Diana whispered again and again. Lane's hips writhed on her thighs in an increasingly frenzied erotic dance, her breathing desperate sobs, her hands clutching at Diana's shoulders. "Oh God," she gasped into Diana's neck as her body suddenly tensed. "Oh God—" Her head jerked violently backward, the sounds in her throat abruptly stilled as her body convulsed with shudders.

Diana, an arm around her shoulders, lowered her to the bed, fingers still within her, feeling powerful tremors continue to pulse against her fingers, hearing the struggle for breath. Her lips brushed Lane's face and the swiftly beating pulse in her throat. "You are so beautiful," she said softly. "Dear God, so very, very beautiful."

Strands of blonde hair lay across Diana's face; as she held Lane she blew on them gently, watching them flutter. It was some time before Lane spoke, and her voice was quiet, near Diana's ear. "Thank you for telling me I was still beautiful to you after that."

"You were. You are."

"When we were having the drink together I was ready for you like that. When we were playing that game. When that man asked me to have a drink—I was ready for you like that."

"Lane," whispered Diana, closing her eyes, her arms tightening.

After a while Lane said, "That had some of the qualities of a sedative, and I don't want to sleep. Would you take a shower with me?"

"Why don't you sleep for a while, let me hold you?"

"I don't want to sleep. I want to take a shower with you."

Diana smiled. Lane's voice had contained the stubbornness of a child.

"It's obligatory," Lane said. "You know, the obligatory shower scene." She smiled coaxingly, her eyes heavy-lidded with tiredness.

"Since it's obligatory," Diana said, kissing her forehead, filled with tenderness, humoring her as she would a child.

Lane stood under cool water. Diana looked at her from the open shower door, at the curving slenderness of her as water streamed off her body. Lane turned the temperature higher and held out her hand.

Diana stood under the spray, Lane leaning against the wall, watching. Then she was in Lane's arms, eyes closed to tender, melting kisses on the bruises on her shoulders.

Lane murmured, "I hope that will make them go away."

Playfully, Diana pushed her away and brushed at her shoulders as if to rub the kisses off. "I like them. I don't want them to go away." Smiling, she slid her arms around Lane's shoulders and stood on tiptoe so that their eyes were level.

Lane laughed. "You're crazy. And lovely. So lovely I can't decide what I like best. The first night I thought it was this." She kissed her mouth lightly. "Then I thought nothing could feel like these." Lane's hands cupped her breasts. "Overflowing my hands. Wonderful, incredible to kiss. Then last night I discovered an altogether new place." Lane's mouth was close to her ear: "It's my current favorite."

"I have no preference," Diana teased. "I love you everywhere."

"Everywhere?"

"Everywhere."

"Kiss my breast. Any breast."

"I don't think I trust you. What do you have in that interesting mind of yours?" She bent to her, and Lane passed the bar of soap in front of her mouth.

"What's the matter? I thought you loved me everywhere."

"You're a tease. A rotten little tease." Diana seized and tickled her.

"I can't stand being tickled!" Lane shrieked convincingly, and Diana stopped. She soaped Diana's body vigorously as Diana squirmed and laughed. "What about you, Diana? Are you ticklish? Are you?" Her fingers probed.

"Of course not," Diana said, gritting her teeth.

"Aha!" Diana had suddenly leaped away from her fingers. "You liar!" Lane grabbed her and moved her body into her, rubbing against the soapsuds lasciviously, eyes sparkling with mischief. "You look cute in soapsuds. Adorable, in fact."

There was the taste of water on Lane's lips, then a tongue that touched Diana's and was gone; then warm breath on her ear, the caressing tip of Lane's tongue; then Lane's mouth on hers again, weakening her with each tongue stroke. Lane's hands moved on her hips, down to her thighs. Diana clung to her. The shower spray stripped the soap from their bodies; Lane held her, kissing her, fingers caressing.

"I want you," Diana breathed, trembling.

Lane moved her to the far wall of the shower. "Tell me again." She knelt to her. "I want to hear you say it."

"Oh God I want you," Diana whispered, eyes tightly shut, her inner thighs quivering, bathed by light warm tongue strokes. Then she arched, as shower spray thrummed on Lane's shoulders, bouncing up into her hair.

* * * * *

"Showers are too small to really maneuver in," Lane said, vigorously toweling her hair. "And the water washes away what you love to taste."

"I liked it," Diana said, her legs still slightly tremulous. She took Lane's towel and patted her dry, drinking some of the translucent drops from Lane's skin.

"Come to bed," Lane said, taking her hand.

Diana took her into her arms as they lay down together. "Let me hold you for a little while."

"I don't want to sleep," Lane said in her stubborn child's voice. "Don't you want what I want?"

Diana said soothingly, "Of course I do." She pulled the sheet up, and drew Lane's face to her breasts, and stroked her hair. "Let's just be warm together for a little while."

Sighing luxuriously, Lane pressed her face into Diana's breasts. Moments later, in total happiness, Diana held Lane's soft body asleep in her arms.

Diana awoke in darkness and picked up her watch from the night table. Nine o'clock.

She sat up, and for a long time gazed at Lane, who slept on her stomach, hands beside her head like a child. Then she stared out the window at the dark shapes of the Sierras, and for the first time in two days, thought of Jack.

How could she love holding the broad shoulders of a man, she wondered, again watching Lane sleep, and these slender shoulders. Love burying her face in the hair on Jack's firm chest, and love to press her face into the incredible softness of Lane's breasts, and breathe in the delicate scents of her. His mouth—so firm, hungry, exciting. Hers—sweet, soft, melting. His arms, his body—insistent, carrying her, sweeping her with him. Her arms, her body—tender, giving, dissolving her. Diffuse, enveloping sensations with him, combined with his own urgency, his excitement. Orgasm with her, strong and pure—eclipse, sometimes lights behind her eyes—with Lane a rapt audience knowing the heights of her ecstasy. Her own rapture when ecstasy flooded Lane, ecstasy that she had given her . . .

Butterfly interlude. The words haunted her. Would Lane simply return to San Francisco, her desire to possess a woman satisfied, and resume her life without a backward glance? Tomorrow assumed a black, terrifying shapelessness, and she turned her thoughts from it.

She contemplated Lane—a beautiful, tender blonde child breathing deeply, slowly, her body moving almost imperceptibly.

You're all I want, she told her in her mind. Seeing you here and knowing I can hold you in my arms is all I want.

She woke Lane, saying her name very softly and kissing her forehead.

"Diana," Lane said sleepily, turning over and reaching for her. "What time is it?"

"Nine-thirty," Diana said, stroking her hair.

Lane held her, kissed her face, her eyes. She sat up, an arm around Diana, and stared at the dark shapes of the mountains. "How did it get to be so late?"

"We'd better get back," Diana said, kissing her cheek.

They dressed. Diana stood by the night table putting on her bracelet, watching Lane at the mirror brush her hair with a few swift, expert strokes. Diana's eyes traveled down her body, lingering on her hips. With a hot surge of pleasure she remembered the night before, the passion of her mouth and hands on Lane, the sounds Lane had made that had been only partly muffled by a pillow.

Lane's eyes met hers in the mirror. "Caught you," she said, and came to her, a half-smile on her lips. Her hands circled Diana's waist. "Exactly what were you thinking about?"

Diana looked at her frankly. "Something I plan to do to you again."

"One of us is a sex maniac."

Diana slid her hands over her shoulders. "Which one?"

Confident of their power to please, they were staring boldly into each other's eyes. Lane smiled, again a half-smile, and kissed Diana, hands moving slowly up her back under her sweater.

Inflamed by cool silk in her hands, against her skin, Diana yielded to tightening arms, her body penetrated by desire, sweet, hot, melting. Lane's hands slid down her back, over her hips; she clasped Diana's hips as their kiss deepened, pressing her hips into her, undulating them. Diana took her mouth away, gasping.

"I am," Lane said, her hands at the belt of Diana's pants.

"We have to get back," Diana said unsteadily. Then she tensed; and soon began to tremble.

Lane lowered her to the bed, drew clothing over her hips, off her body, and knelt beside the bed. She whispered, "Oh God, Diana . . ."

Diana moaned, and her legs rose, to wrap around cool silk.

They sped down Highway 50 toward the cabin. Diana, head back against the headrest watching Lane drive, noticed her scrutiny of restaurants along the road. She asked, "Are you hungry?"

"Starving. I was about to ask you."

"Me too," Diana said, realizing that she was ravenous.

"Thank God. I thought you were going to tell me again we have to get back."

"I have only the vaguest recollection of saying that. Somehow I must've known you were going to make the world fall apart in flaming pieces."

Lane laughed, low, pleased laughter. "How about some junk food?" She gestured at a McDonald's sign looming along the Highway.

"I'm a junk food junkie," Lane said a few minutes later, munching contentedly on her hamburger. "However nutritionally unsound that may be."

"Do you cook?" Diana asked, looking at her in amusement.

"When I have time. I like to sometimes. Do you?"

"Yes. I had to when I was married, when I lived with Jack. But I like to, even for myself."

"McDonald's french fries are the greatest in the world," Lane said, crumpling an empty carton. "Do you like living by yourself?"

"Not really. I've needed to, for a while. Do you . . . live by yourself?"

"I do now. It's easier, overall."

A question surfaced in Diana's mind. She asked casually, "What was Carol like?"

Lane glanced at her. "What do you want to know?"

"What kind of person was she?"

"She was eighteen. I don't think anybody's terribly interesting at eighteen."

Diana was disturbed by her evasiveness. "What did she look like?"

Lane sipped from her Coke before she answered. "Tall, dark hair, dark eyes."

"Was she pretty?"

"Unusually. She reached the finals of the Junior Miss Beauty Pageant."

"Oh." Dismally, Diana bit into her hamburger.

"Carol's mother pushed her into things like that. It was criminal, it turned Carol completely narcissistic about her looks, she spent an amount of time you wouldn't believe on herself." Lane sipped again from her Coke. "Father always called Carol's mother a barbarian. He told me a thousand times physical beauty is grotesquely overvalued in our society, and those who possess it are more cursed than blessed."

"Do you agree with that?"

"Absolutely. It was the origin of all my little games. To find out who saw me as a person and who wanted to wear me as an ornament."

Diana asked suddenly, impulsively, "Lane, do you care for me?"

Lane looked at her. "Your courage simply astounds me."

"I don't know why you keep saying that. When we were first in the motel today, what you trusted me with was an act of total courage."

Lane said pensively, "I guess . . . that's true. I wouldn't have . . . anyone else. But you've taught me a lot about courage and trusting the past few days."

"Are you going to answer my question?"

"Yes. But not right now. And not here. Right now I want to move the car." She gestured toward an empty section of the parking lot.

Lane switched off the ignition and took Diana's hand, holding it on her thigh, lacing their fingers together. "Can you eat with one hand?"

"Easily," Diana said, smiling.

Her hand lay on Lane's thigh as they drove toward the cabin. She moved her fingers inside, feeling warmth and firmness through the fabric.

"I'm going to drive us right off the road," Lane said.

Diana removed her hand and Lane said, "Don't take it away, just don't move it like that. You must know by now what you do to me." She glanced over as Diana's hand again rested on her thigh. "Your hand is so warm. You're so warm. You make me very happy," she said meditatively, steering the car around the curves of the dark mountain. "Happy in more ways than the physical."

"The physical between us is incredible," Diana murmured.

"Yes."

"Do you suppose it's often this good between women?"

Lane's hand, gloveless, cool from the steering wheel, covered and pressed Diana's hand into the warmth of her thigh. "I only know it is for us."

They arrived at the cabin just before eleven o'clock, and learned that Madge had left that afternoon.

"She took it into her head to get back early and surprise Arthur," Liz said. "I hope Arthur doesn't get really surprised. I suggested she might call from Placerville. I hope she does." Liz chuckled. "I bet you my chastity belt Arthur's got somebody helping him with all that room to breathe."

"I wonder if she'll call," Lane mused.

"Who knows," Liz said. "Do you handle divorces?"

Grinning, Lane shook her head.

"Did you girls have a good day?" Chris asked.

"A beautiful day," Lane said.

"Lane has all the makings of a riverboat gambler," Diana said.

"So how do you stand?" Millie asked Lane. "Ahead or behind," she added impatiently as Lane looked at her blankly.

"Uh, I think maybe fifty dollars ahead."

"That's about right," Diana said, smiling.

"Why don't you tell us all about it while Diana's in the bathroom?" Chris said.

"Yes, why don't you," Diana said with a mischievous smile as Lane glanced at her in alarm. "Tell them all about Benny the dealer."

"Oh. Yes."

When she returned, Lane was sitting by the fire holding a glass of wine she had not touched, listening to gambling stories.

"Bathroom's all yours," Diana said, and Lane rose and excused herself, handing her the glass of wine with a look of brimming amusement.

Lane lowered the trapdoor. "You really threw me to the wolves, didn't you, Miss Holland. Without a qualm."

"You're a lawyer, Miss Christianson. Can't you talk your way out of anything? Anything?"

They were sitting on the bed, Diana's head on Lane's shoulder.

"Thank God they started talking about some of their own gambling stories," Lane said, her hands under Diana's pajamas and gentle on her body.

"I knew that would happen. People who gamble can talk about it for hours."

They kissed lingeringly, holding hands. "It's been a whole hour since I've been able to touch you," Lane murmured. "I must say I don't like it, not being able to touch you." She cupped Diana's face. "You made me sleep today and I needed to. We both needed to. You take good care of me."

"I like taking care of you. We have a lot of time to talk, now."

"Or whatever else it may occur to us to do."

Evasive tactics again, Diana thought unhappily.

But Lane said, "Let's arrange the bed so we can talk."

They pulled the blanket off, and after some experimentation, Lane sat propped against pillows with Diana lying on a pillow in her lap, the quilt covering both of them.

"A snug igloo," Lane said approvingly.

"Perfect," Diana said, stroking her hair. "Talk to me about you. About your work. What's your office like?"

"It's nice. Father helped me furnish it. It's in tones of gold and brown, I've got a few good pieces, a Queen Anne chair, an antique table, two good paintings. I have Father's desk now, I'm very proud to have it. I like the office at night. There's a different kind of silence at night, a hush, and the city is incredibly beautiful."

"I'd like to see your office. I love your city." As Lane remained silent, Diana said, "Tell me about the people you work with."

Lane gave her brief character sketches, many of them amusing, of the men with whom she worked, and spoke of problems and projects she had been involved with. "I hate to lose," she said. "It torments me for weeks. I always think if I'd worked harder, prepared more, presented my facts better . . . I *hate* to lose." She talked about law school. "Are you sure you're interested in all this?" she asked again.

"Absolutely. It's fascinating. I don't care how influential your father was, I think you were born to do what you do."

Lane talked quietly, often looking abstractedly out the window as she formed her thoughts into words, her fingers moving caressingly in Diana's hair; she paused sometimes to touch her face to Diana's, her breath light and warm. She talked about her childhood in Oklahoma, growing up in California.

"This is your life, Lane Christianson," she joked, "God, I've never talked this much in my life. I want to hear about you. Tell me about your work."

"There's not much to tell. I want to get into personnel administration. I finally finished college three years ago, but my life was too bound up with Jack and I guess there was a lot of inertia—it's so easy to stay with what you know. I don't feel that way now. There are so many possibilities, so many exciting things . . . I feel like Madge's giraffe, my long neck up to see what's going on around me."

Lane smiled and kissed her, tender kisses on her eyes, her lips.

Diana whispered, her eyes still closed, "You have the sweetest, softest, tenderest mouth."

A fingertip touched, traced Diana's lips. "Your lips feel rich and soft to mine. Tell me about things you like. What kinds of books do you like?"

They talked about books, and music. Lane stroked Diana's hair, traced her face.

"You're such a pretty woman," Lane told her. "Delicate, soft features. Everything about you is soft and curving, even the way your hair curls around your face. Tell me about a day in your life. In a minute." They kissed slowly, deeply, for a long time, Diana's hands caressing her shoulders.

Diana talked about her daily activities, her life in Los Angeles. Lane's fingers stroked her throat, unbuttoned her pajama top to caress her shoulders, to caress where the swelling of her breasts began. Desire had long since begun, long since heightened; she was no longer surprised at how easily or how much she desired Lane.

"Tell me about where you live, describe it to me." Fingernails brushed lightly in the hollow of Diana's throat, across to her shoulders.

"You're making it difficult for me to talk."

"I know. I can hear it in your voice. I want to hear it, how you feel when I touch you. Is that all right?"

"Yes. If I can."

"Your throat is so soft, your shoulders are so warm and pretty. Tell me about where you live."

"A small apartment building in the Valley, very quiet, one bedroom, a small dining room . . ."

As she continued to speak, Lane looked into her eyes and stroked her arms, inside her elbows, her wrists; she kissed her fingers, her hands. "Your hands are so soft and sweet," Lane said, "so feminine, your arms around me are always so warm, they have such sweet, delicate places to touch, kiss. Tell me what colors there are in your bedroom. Describe it to me exactly."

"The walls are creamy white. My bedspread is deep blue. I have pictures of the ocean along one wall . . ."

Lane's hands held her breasts, long supple fingers curved around them. She looked directly into Diana's eyes. Diana spoke with effort through her pleasure.

"What's your favorite color?" Lane asked, fingertips gliding lightly, rhythmically over her nipples.

"Gray . . . blue," breathed Diana.

"Not blue-gray?" Lane smiled.

Diana spoke more easily as the fingers left her nipples to caress her breasts again. "No, there's more gray than blue," she said, looking into her eyes.

"Some things just can't be described," Lane said in a low, musing voice. "The firmness, the heavenly softness of your breasts. How they shape themselves to my hands. Beautiful, so beautiful . . . Diana, tell me where you would live if you could."

"On the ocean."

"Describe it to me. The house you'd like to have on the ocean."

Diana said, "It would be right on the beach. There would be tall windows . . . all the way . . . down to the floor. And . . . a fireplace . . . near the windows so you could . . . look at the fire . . . and the water." Lane's mouth left one breast, came to the other. "And there would be . . . books all over the walls. And . . . a thick carpet . . . for us . . ." Diana held Lane's mouth to her.

"Diana."

"Yes," she whispered.

"Look at me. Tell me how you feel."

Diana opened her eyes. The lids were swollen, heavy. "Like . . . whipped cream all over inside."

"You have a lovely tender place just around, close to your nipples, I love kissing there. I love your breasts, kissing them. There's only one other place I kiss where I can tell so well the pleasure I give . . ." She kissed Diana's body, her hands sliding Diana's pajamas down over her hips. "It's a sense of power I love . . . Diana?"

"Yes." She lay nude, breathing deeply with her sensations, Lane's hands and lips and tongue caressing her body, silk hair brushing her skin.

"Your lovely body . . . Every time I take you in my arms you melt into me . . . And so soft to my hands, sweet to my lips . . . Tell me about your house at the ocean. Tell me about the bedroom. What color is it?"

"Blue . . . different shades . . . of blue." She shuddered from Lane's hands, her mouth, inside her thighs.

"Velvet . . . I could touch, kiss here forever. How you tremble . . . your soft hair . . . Tell me about our bedroom, Diana. Talk to me . . . Tell me about our bedroom."

"Glass . . . down to . . . the floor . . . and . . . a fireplace . . ."

"Oh God so sweet . . . Diana . . . Talk . . ."

"Lane . . ."

She spoke in halting whispers, awkwardly, with many pauses as she searched for words. "Streams, rivers of feeling. Then it's like hot liquid brimming on the edge, ready to overflow, ready, ready, and oh God it does, pours all through me, flows everywhere at once, into my throat, down my legs and my arms and into my wrists. Everywhere, everything in me . . . glows. Your mouth is heaven," she finished, and was angry with herself for trying to describe what she could not describe, for the poverty of her words. But Lane's arms abruptly tightened, an unaware, painful tightening.

"Lane, what do I taste like?"

Lane was silent for a while; she stroked Diana's hair. "It's more than taste. It's how you feel—like satin in places, and . . . intricate. And it's like smelling trees and flowers, and earth, and rain. The taste . . . how can I—" She suddenly smiled. "I know. Our Emily wrote about hummingbird drunk with nectar. 'I taste a liquor never brewed.' The taste of you, Diana."

"You're like ocean to me."

"Like . . . salt?"

"Maybe a trace. I don't know. I can't explain it any more than that. It's like being at the ocean. It's lovely."

Diana disengaged herself from Lane, and sat up. "Why won't you talk about what happens afterward? Am I a butterfly interlude for you, Lane?"

"No. But I think I may very well be for you."

Diana sat still in shock; then shook her head in bewilderment. "I don't understand."

"We've both discovered things about ourselves the last few days. But your discovery is different from mine. You know now that a woman is possible for you. I've discovered that for me a woman is necessary."

"I don't understand at all."

"I mean that you've just discovered the idea of sexuality with another woman, but you haven't looked at any of the realities."

"Yes I have." Diana thought of the ordeal that had led her to Chick Benson. "Problems can be worked out if we want to . . . to be together."

"You haven't even considered what you're saying, Diana. You haven't had time. Not really. I know. I've lived with myself for fifteen years. You're confusing knowledge with courage."

"I'm more than just a sexual being, Lane."

"That's exactly the point."

"And I'm not a child, either. I'm thirty-four years old."

"You have many needs—and options."

Diana said vehemently, "I can't stand euphemisms, especially from you. I want you. You."

"I'm only asking that you think about it."

With a feeling of desperation Diana said, "I don't need to think about it. I know how I feel. I can tell you that right now."

Lane raised a hand in a gesture of command. "No. Not until you're away from stars and snow—and this room—for a while."

"From you."

"For a while."

"Do you need to think about me?"

"It's different for me. I know now that Mark was an accident for me—as I am for you."

"I think this is possible for anyone."

Lane sighed. "Many things are possible for people, the labels they attach are senseless. But our opinion won't change reality. I want you to take the time to think about this, about me, in context with your life. When you're with your family, your friends. When you're making plans about your career. I've told you how my father would have reacted to a relationship like ours. What would your father think?"

"Dad's always told me I had all the intelligence I needed to make good decisions about my life, and I should always consider my own happiness."

"Would this make him happy?"

Diana hesitated. "It's my life, Lane."

"What about your friends? Vivian? The people you work with?"

"It's my life," Diana repeated stubbornly.

"That's what I'm saying, too. I only want you to carefully consider your own happiness."

"How long do you want me to take?"

"I think a month."

"A month!" Diana said, appalled. "Without seeing you? Can I talk to you?"

Lane shook her head. "I may be something you get over like an attack of measles. A virulent attack," she said with a smile that was prideful. "You're on the rebound from a man you cared for, you may simply go back to him—or to some other man—and put me in your scrapbook as one of your more interesting and unusual affairs. There may be a psychological factor involved you're not aware of, something connected to your early life that caused you to need a woman, you may have met that need now, worked through it. You might even want to talk to a psychologist to get some insight into your feelings."

"A month is forever," Diana said insistently. "It's such a long time!"

"After the first night with you, when I knew I would come to you again, all that day I thought of an Emily Dickinson line: 'I had been hungry all the years.'" Lane looked at her for a long moment. "All those years for me, Diana. I only want you to take a month. One month. To consider whether this is right for you."

"I've been hungry all the years too, Lane. Waiting for Lane Christianson the person, whether that would be a man or a woman."

"I accept the fact," Lane said quietly, "that I prefer Diana Holland to be a woman."

Diana said, "What if I don't need the whole month?"

Lane smiled. "A month, Diana. The Emily Dickinson poem goes on to say that hunger for some things ends, the entering takes away. If the entering hasn't taken away, there are a lot of years."

She'll never make me wait the whole month, Diana thought. "All right," she said.

"You call me four weeks from today. Thursday. At seven that night. Agreed?"

She'll never make me wait, Diana thought. "Agreed."

"I have something for you." Lane opened the drawer of the night table. "I found it this morning when I was making my phone calls." She gave Diana a black velvet jewelers box.

Diana accepted the box, looking at Lane wonderingly. She opened it, turned it to the starlight. Lying in the black velvet interior was a delicate silver cross on a fine silver chain. Diamonds glittered, one on each end of the cross. "The Southern Cross," Diana whispered.

"I had to get it for you. You can have your own to look at till you get to see the real one. I was so happy to find this, I noticed it right away in the case. It was all by itself on a black velvet tray."

"Lane . . . it's absolutely beautiful." Diana stared at it, turning the box in her hands, gazing at the soft glow of silver and the sparkle of diamonds. "It looks very expensive."

"It is. Does that bother you?"

She considered. "No, I'm too happy to have it. Unless it was an extravagant impulse you really can't afford."

"I can afford it. Shall I put it on you?"

"I wish I had something for you. I wish I could give you your fantasy of running naked through the rain."

Lane smiled. "Think about it, Diana. Haven't I been running naked, with rain on my face?"

Diana gave Lane the box, watched her fingers lift the cross and chain from the black folds of velvet. Lane fastened the chain around Diana's neck, holding the cross, and kissed the place just below Diana's throat where the cross rested when she released it.

"It's very beautiful on you," she said.

Diana touched Lane's face and kissed her gently. "Thank you, Lane."

"You're welcome," Lane said huskily, her eyes closed.

Diana said with careful casualness, "I suppose I'll have to pay for this now. You didn't give it to me with purely platonic intentions, did you?"

Lane looked away, but her lips twitched with the beginning of a smile. "I haven't had a single platonic intention toward you for some time."

"Isn't this what's known as taking it out in trade?"

Lane looked at her, smiling. "I'm afraid so. I'll have to take the cross off, first. It could puncture you if we're not careful. And I don't intend to be careful."

"Are you sure you won't just go back to San Francisco and take up with one of those willing women?"

"Do I detect signs of a jealous woman?"

"I never used to be. I never thought I was anything like Liz, either, but if you so much as look at another woman—"

"I like you jealous," Lane said as she lowered the cross into its black velvet box. "But it's not necessary."

Diana sighed. "Now to get those pajamas off you. My own way," she added, pushing Lane's hands away from the buttons of her pajamas. She took Lane into her arms and said teasingly, "I think I'll have you describe things, too. First your apartment, then—"

"I couldn't, Diana," Lane said seriously. "It's all I can do to breathe."

Diana held Lane's face in her hands, smoothed blonde hair back, kissed her forehead. "Fair is fair." She slid her arms around her and lowered her into pillows. "I plan to kiss you from head to toe, with a long slow stop at a place in between. Could I at least have a moan or two?"

"Moans I can guarantee," Lane whispered.

Thank you for everything, Liz," Diana said. "I can't thank you enough."

The women were all outside the cabin: Liz and Chris and Millie ready to leave for the ski slopes, Lane at her car arranging luggage in the trunk.

Liz beamed. "It was great having you here, Diana. I'm glad you had a good time."

"Please call when you come to Los Angeles. I have so much hospitality to repay."

"Not at all. I hope to see you in San Francisco."

"I'd love it." She exchanged goodbyes with Millie and Chris, shaking hands with Millie, hugging Chris. She took Lane's hands without speaking.

Lane looked at her for a long moment, squeezed her hands and released them, and turned and got into her car.

She followed Lane's car down the mountain road. At the intersection of Highway 50, before turning onto the Highway, Lane looked back at her, rolled down her window. "Diana?" she called.

"Yes," Diana answered with wild hope.

"Take care, Diana."

"And you, Lane." She watched until the tiny silver car disappeared. Then she turned onto the Highway and drove to Harrah's to pick up Vivian.

"I'll take us to Placerville," Vivian said, "then we can switch off. We'd better switch off pretty often, honey. We're both pretty tired."

"I don't feel tired." She felt empty, of everything but misery, and doubt.

"Buster, would you move your molasses ass," Vivian growled at the truck crawling along in front of them. "When's the next passing lane?"

"I think another four miles," Diana said absently. "Tell me something, Viv. Hypothetical question. Let's suppose a . . . Jewish girl falls in love with . . . a black man. She falls in love kind of by accident, without really being able to help it, and—"

"I would think so," Vivian interrupted. "If she had any sense at all. Who needs that?"

Diana ignored Vivian, concentrating on her choice of words. "They make love, and he doesn't tell her he cares for her in so many words, but he acts like he really does, everything he does strongly indicates he really does. He gives her an expensive gift, tells her to take a month to think things over to be sure of her feelings, to be sure it's worth the problems their relationship would cause. Do you think he means it?" She added hurriedly, as Vivian stared at her, "It's an argument we had at the cabin."

"Crazy argument," Vivian said, looking straight ahead again, tailgating the truck. "The answer is no, he doesn't mean it. The expensive gift is the best clue—that's always the big kiss-off. If you want somebody bad enough, devil take the consequences. That other kind of love—the kind where somebody loves somebody so much they'll risk losing them—that belongs in books."

Dismayed by her answer, Diana remonstrated, "Well, I think it's possible."

"You haven't lived long enough. One thing for sure, your hypothetical Jewish girl will find out in a month." Vivian chuckled. "If she calls and he can't remember her name, I'd say she's in trouble. You had some pretty strange arguments there at the cabin."

"Yes." Trying to reassure herself, Diana took her cross from under her sweater, fingers caressing metal warm from her skin.

Vivian swung the car out and passed the truck with a surge of horsepower. "Go drive that truck in your cabbage patch, you dumb son of a bitch," she screamed, lifting her middle finger. As she eased the car over into the right hand lane, she glanced over at Diana.

"Diana! What are you doing with that? I saw Lane Christianson buy that yesterday at Harrah's."

"I have it on loan," Diana blurted, certain she had gone white.

"On loan?" Vivian said incredulously, braking sharply for a curve. "That's the craziest thing I ever heard of. That's *real.* The counter she was at doesn't sell fake diamonds."

"She insisted." Thinking frantically she added, "She bought it for . . . a cousin in . . . in Laguna Beach—"

"A *cousin?*"

"I . . . No, it was a sister," Diana said desperately. "She'll be down later this month to give it to her, it's safer if I keep it—"

"That I can believe," Vivian said. "San Francisco's changed so much, you couldn't pay me to live there. That's a pretty expensive gift for a sister."

Diana said, making her voice carefully neutral, "Why? She has money. She's a lawyer, she drives a Mercedes."

"I suppose so. But even so, a sister—"

Diana said hurriedly, "Lane didn't mention seeing you at Harrah's."

"I mentioned it yesterday when I saw you both, remember? She was very closed-mouthed when I mentioned it, and she was acting damn odd when she bought it, too."

"Odd?"

"Like she was in another world. You know how curious Vivian is, I went over to see what she was buying. I spoke to her, she looked right through me like I wasn't even there. She sure is one good-looking woman."

"Yes."

"Liz told me she goes through men like a lawn mower goes through grass. Madge calls her Venus Mantrap."

Diana laughed, relieved at the change in direction of their conversation. "So?" she said indifferently. It occurred to her that she was unconcerned about the men that Lane had been with—so long as she was the only woman.

"She a nympho?"

"What kind of question is that?" Diana asked, astonished. "And how should I know?"

"You spent time together. What did you talk about?"

"Astronomy, law, music, books." She added, smiling, "Architecture, interior decorating."

"Jesus. With looks like hers, all those men—I figure she's nympho. Or she'd be married."

"Why aren't you married? Why am I not married?"

"Don't get so feisty, what the hell do I care?" Vivian swerved around a curve. "This goddamn one horse highway, you'd think they'd do something about it." She continued in a quiet voice, "Diana dear, I'm sorry as hell about that bastard you met up here."

"Don't worry about it, forget it. I'll be grateful all my life you talked me into coming up here."

"That's pretty extravagant." Vivian's tone was pleased, and slightly puzzled.

"I mean it."

"You feel better about Jack?"

"I feel better about me. From now on I intend to be possessive about what I love. To fight to keep it."

"You don't mean that about Jack, do you?"

"I mean it generally."

"I hope you've learned to look at him a little more coldly and see he's no great loss. When a thirty-eight year old man just wants to play golf all weekend you begin to suspect he still has his rubber duck."

Diana chuckled. "I bow to your superior wisdom, Viv."

"Vivian knows whereof she speaks."

As Vivian continued to talk, Diana fingered the cross at her throat, pondering how close she had come to not being able to think of a lie. She was not accustomed to lying. And there would be no end to the lies to protect herself and those she loved—and Lane. Lane had asked her to consider their relationship in context with her life. Could she accept the lying, deception, pretense? Soberly, she contemplated the courage required for people to come out of the closet of secrecy she had just walked into. What kind of courage did she have? How strong was she?

That evening, back home at her apartment, she found a note in her mail.

Diana,
    Your department secretary told me you're at Tahoe. I promise not to bother you ever again if you see me one time. I'll be at your apartment Monday night at eight unless I hear from you.
    Please see me. I need you to do this for me.

                                                    JACK

Depressed, Diana unpacked and immediately went to bed. She fell asleep remembering the motel on the Lake, and Lane's tender body, the texture of gold hair on her breasts as Lane slept in her arms.

At exactly eight o'clock the following Monday night, Diana opened her apartment door to Jack Gordon.

Warm feeling surged through her at the sight of him, but she was immensely relieved when he made no attempt to touch her. "Come in. Can I get you something to drink? Scotch?"

"Okay, if you have something to mix it with. To tell you the truth, I never did like how it tastes."

"I knew that." She looked at him in surprise. He had always drunk his liquor with water, and without pleasure, always referring to mixed drinks as fag drinks.

"How was vacation? Were you lucky?"

"A little. It's a beautiful place."

"Yeah, I remember. You wanted to go back, and we should have. You look fantastic, Diana. Better than I've ever seen you look."

"Thank you. How about vodka and ginger ale? You might like that."

He nodded, and followed her into the kitchen, watched her pour his drink. "Nice place," he said glancing around. "You've really fixed it up. You're awfully good at stuff like that."

"Thanks. And you look good, too," she told him. "Very sharp, in fact." He was freshly barbered, and wore a light gray suit, a white shirt, a subtly striped tie. He looked crisp and handsome.

In the living room they sat across from each other. Jack made conversation about his relatives, other people they knew. Diana listened with detachment and an impatience she soon realized was boredom.

Jack paused, and in the silence between them, cleared his throat. "I wanted you to know I've been seeing a psychiatrist. I started to go from bad to worse over this, the way I screwed up something so good. I'll tell you the truth, why I went to him. To find out if he could help me get you back."

A hand at her throat, she studied him.

He continued, "So I've been seeing him three weeks now, four times a week. He showed me what a prick I've been. I learned a lot about myself I didn't like learning, but it was all true. It's about time I grew up, Diana. He asked me questions about you I couldn't answer. What you think about things. What kind of books you read. Jesus, I didn't know. After five years of living with you, loving you. I'm not proud of how I was with you. I was a jerk."

Nonplussed, she stared at him.

"I've been a lot more serious since you . . . since we broke up. I guess they were looking for some clue I was settling down. Richardson recommended me for sales manager."

She said excitedly, delighted for him, "Jack, that's wonderful. You'll be so good, you have such skill with people—"

His smile was warm and eager. "Thanks, honey. But there's one hitch. I'll be transferred, the Florida office. Fort Lauderdale. I'll be leaving in another week."

"I see." She felt pummeled by tiny shocks.

"I've thought about it, I talked to Doctor Phipps. I've decided I want to go. If we don't get back together I think it's better for me to get away. If we do, it would be good to start again in a new place. So I can show you I've really grown up." He looked at her beseechingly. "Florida isn't a bad place. And if I do a good job I won't be there more than a year. Two at the most. And we could come back right away if we hated it."

"I'm sure Florida isn't a bad place," she murmured.

"I want you to come with me, start all over again. I'd really like us to get married, but if you don't want to, that's okay. I want you to come with me. Diana — give me one more chance."

Diana said without pain and with utter certainty, "No, Jack."

Jack sighed, looked down at his drink, rattled the ice cubes. "Think it over. Take a couple of days."

"I don't need to."

"I love you, Diana. I need you." His eyes, his voice were pleading.

She said resignedly, hating this, knowing it was inevitable, "You need someone. Not necessarily me. You can love a lot of women. Maybe you should."

"You're the only woman I want. Nobody else ever meant anything. You loved me once. You know you did."

"It isn't enough."

"There were so many good things. Remember? The good things? Breakfast in bed? Reading the paper to each other? Remember Bourbon Street? The way we discovered it together? Remember how good it all was? Our trips to Vegas? Christmas at Yosemite? Jesus it was so pretty. Our friends want us back together. Bud and Rita miss us at Friday night poker."

"It isn't enough."

"It was so good in bed, you know it was. We're terrific for each other. Doctor Phipps says not many people have sex as good as we did, as often. After five years, to still want it that much, it was a very good thing we had together."

"It isn't enough."

"You've got somebody already. Is that it, Diana?"

She touched the cross at her throat, hidden in the folds of her dress. "I feel no need to answer that question."

"There *is* somebody."

She shrugged. "I've already answered that question."

He picked up his drink. A drop fell from the frosted glass onto the table. She thought of slender fingers stroking frost from a glass. He rubbed the drop carefully with his fingers, removing it from the table, and put the drink down.

"It's really over, then?"

Diana nodded. "Yes," she said.

He said, "The doctor said sometimes when love ends it just ends. There's nothing left, the spark goes out, it's just over."

Diana did not reply.

He said, "I don't know if that's true but I guess there's no point in hashing things over. I'm a good salesman, but you know the product I'm trying to sell you, you had it for five years. I'm just telling you again it's a new improved product. I'll be around another week if you change your mind."

He rose. His strides toward the door slowed, stopped. "Can we stay friends?"

"Yes. But I think our lives will be quite separate." She opened the door, wanting him to be quickly gone. She was close to tears.

"Let me kiss you?"

"No, Jack. Don't try," she ordered sharply as he moved toward her.

"Am I that repulsive now?" His face was twisted with hurt, anger.

"No," she said, in pain. "There's just no reason to."

"Good luck," he said abruptly. "You know where I am."

"Good luck to you."

In a desolation of loneliness, she stood by her living room window, wiping tears away, remembering tender lips kissing her eyes and moving down to warmly, sweetly wash tears from her face. She turned and stared at the telephone she would use three weeks and three nights from tonight, longing for the time to be past, tormented by the possibility her call might not even be answered.

She watched Jack's car roar away, the headlights quickly

vanishing in the night. There was a scent of burning wood in the spring air, someone's fireplace. Diana drew the scent into her lungs, thinking it could be the smell of burning bridges.

She went to bed early each night, slept late on weekends. In a twilight state of half-sleep she would lie in bed for hours, her mind gliding through a gallery of memories, lengthy episodes, brief scenes, still pictures, an unending flow of her time with Lane. She caught and held moments in timeless dreaming memory: the concentrated intelligence in Lane's eyes as she articulated a thought; Lane smiling; Lane's face in the shadows of their room; a scene of their lovemaking—Lane's face, her lips very full and parted as she breathed in deep gasps, her eyes tightly closed, masking emotion from Diana in unsharing privacy as orgasm drained from her.

Soon she had trouble concentrating on Lane's face; when she tried to hold it in sharp focus it became ambiguously featured. Bitterly, she reproached herself for not having a picture of Lane. Her clearest images now emerged from other people: an element of someone's features, the line of body, a stride, the curve of hair over a forehead—these would bring sudden breath-taking images that would begin to fade even as she focused on them.

She was acutely conscious of her own body, examining herself hypercritically—her figure, her skin and muscle tone. She groomed her hair and nails endlessly and began to exercise, performing for an hour each day a strenuous regimen that left her in limp exhaustion, muscles trembling. In the evenings she walked, long walks, her mind shrouded, lulled by the rhythmic cadence of her footsteps. Then the thought occurred that Lane might call—impulsively, perhaps. Rationally, she knew that Lane was too disciplined, too highly controlled; nevertheless, she stopped walking in the evenings.

For a week after she saw Jack, she paced and stalked her apartment, smoldering with anger. If Lane cared anything about her she would relent, break their agreement and call. Lane was putting her through this, making her wait and suffer, giving her this anguish, these doubts.

During the weekdays she occupied her mind with her job, striving for perfection in her paperwork, immersing herself during interviews. In the evenings, unable to concentrate on television or reading except for brief periods, unable to listen to music, which she had discovered tormented her, she cooked elaborate dishes requiring considerable effort and attention. She would eat her creations absently and without interest as she glanced over a newspaper or magazine. The importance of these meals was solely in their preparation.

Three weeks after their return from Lake Tahoe, Vivian took her to lunch and chided her with grumpy affection. "You won't come over, you won't even talk to me on the phone. I know I'm a big bore but you could at least be polite for the sake of the years we've been friends. God, Diana . . . I thought maybe it would be better once we got back from Tahoe."

Diana said contritely, "I'll be better soon. I just need to be by myself for now. Why don't you just leave me be and stop worrying?"

"I can't do that, honey. You're alone there in that apartment." Vivian took Diana's hand, rubbed it between her two. "Dear," she said worriedly, "people who won't see or talk to other people often develop . . . problems. Diana honey, they can even have nervous breakdowns."

"Oh Viv, please don't worry," Diana said, stricken with guilt. "It's not anything remotely like that. I just need a little more time. Then things will be . . . will change, I promise."

Vivian said doubtfully, "Well, okay. At least I see you every day at the office."

As time dragged by, Diana was tortured by an increasing conviction that Lane's feeling would not survive their separation, that too many factors were working against it. Five days and nights together was too little time. Their relationship was too tenuous and too perilous to last. Lane would become immersed in her work, all her emotion and energy again channeled into her career. Her father's influence would reach out to her, reassert itself—even from the grave his disapproval would cause Lane to relinquish once more her strongest desires.

Thoughts of Carol haunted her. Jealousy was a new emotion, and it savaged her. Carol would be thirty-three now, undoubtedly very beautiful still—perhaps more so; some women became more beautiful with age. Did Lane still care for her even after the interval of years? Would she seek her, released from the inhibitions that had prevented a relationship she had desired so much? Diana thought of Carol incessantly as she exercised, as she shaped and polished her fingernails, as she creamed her skin and brushed her hair, thinking of her in a violent jealous hatred.

Intermittently and with pain, she thought of Jack. He had called her once, before he had left for Florida, pleading, finally breaking down, crying. He had never cried before with her. She had been calm; she had taken his new address in Fort Lauderdale as if it had been information given her by a stranger. Afterward she had lain on her sofa for hours, remembering him and crying, the memory of his sobs stabbing into her, and feeling utterly alone and more unhappy than she ever had in her life.

She could bear least of all the empty expanses of weekends, and she fled from her aloneness to her father. She spent three Sundays at his house, going over early in the day, staying into the evening, watching TV sports with him, cooking for him, playing games of cribbage, listening to stories of his teaching, reminiscing over their lives together.

The last Sunday before she would call Lane was a soft mild day in April. That afternoon she sat with her father at the picnic table in his backyard, playing cards. As she picked up the deck to shuffle for another game of cribbage, his large gentle hands covered hers.

"You know I never interfere," he said.

"I don't know if I've ever deserved your confidence," she said, relaxed and warm under his affection, "but I've always appreciated it."

"Non-interference has been difficult at times—especially when you were married. But you were an adult . . ." He took his hands away, reached into the pocket of his plaid shirt for his pipe. "I've been seeing a lot of you lately, not that I haven't loved you being here — "

"I'm really fine, Dad," she murmured, lowering her eyes. "There's nothing wrong."

He lit his pipe, tamping the tobacco down as he applied flame. She had never understood how he managed not to burn his index finger.

"Several coincidences concern me, my love. Jack, for one. I'll confess to you now, I had many misgivings about him all the time you lived together. I do like a man who marries his woman, gives her all the protection he can. For a liberal democrat, I do have my old-fashioned quirks. But Jack showed me a new, mature side of him. He asked me to help him with you. Of course I couldn't, wouldn't . . . But I'll always have more respect for him."

She remained silent, watching her father stroke his gray goatee with a thumb and middle finger, a habitual gesture. As he sucked on his pipe, he studied her with light brown eyes the same shape as her own.

"Then Vivian called. For Vivian to call . . ." He sighed. "Well, she's a good friend to both of us but it's you she truly loves. Those two events, and you coming over so much. For a grown child to suddenly need to be with a parent . . ." He sighed again. "Whatever's wrong, I know it isn't Jack. I know how damaging your divorce was to your self-esteem . . . I don't believe Jack can even compare to that. I want you to tell me what's wrong."

Diana riffled the cards, reflecting. She could not tell her father — but what could she say to him? "Dad," she finally said, "I won't lie to you and insist nothing's wrong. But I'm all right, I really am." She smiled — disarmingly, she hoped. "I respectfully request a return to your non-interference policy."

He smiled, pushed a shock of brown-gray hair off his forehead. "There were things I didn't tell my parents, either. Especially as a young man. But those were different times, and we're two mature, intelligent people, more sophisticated than most. There isn't much in this world that would even surprise me, let alone disturb me."

She hesitated, still riffling the cards, studying her father anxiously, uncertainly. He put his pipe down on the picnic table, covered her hands again with his. "I know you. Nothing you can say would . . . disturb me."

"Dad," she said, seizing all her courage and looking into his eyes, "what if I told you I've fallen in love with a woman?"

He looked down, at their hands. He turned her hands over, and for some time rubbed his palms against hers. "When you turned sixteen," he said, his eyes on hers, but distant, "I began to prepare myself. I thought about you bringing home a black man, a Chicano, a bearded orthodox Jew—"

She began to chuckle.

"—I even imagined a young man with hair down to his waist and playing a sitar." His smile was sudden, and self-mocking. "I don't know why it never occurred to me to prepare myself for—"

He released her hands, picked up his pipe. "I need a little time . . . Do you know why this . . ." He looked at her helplessly.

"I've never known what it is that I needed, or even that I needed. Until I found this."

"Is it . . . is it because after your mother . . ." He swallowed and said with difficulty, "Because I never gave you another—"

She gripped his arms. "Oh Dad, no. That's crazy. Most children don't get the love from two parents that I got from you."

"Baby," he said. "But why—now? Unless . . . you and Barbara?"

"No." She admitted, "Maybe it . . . could have. But it just didn't."

"This . . . this love isn't making you happy. The opposite."

"What's making me unhappy isn't how I feel, it's being uncertain how she feels. She's insisted on a separation. To . . . examine my feelings."

"How long have you known her?"

"About . . . a month."

Visibly relaxing, he picked up his pipe and puffed, to conceal a smile, she judged.

"Dad," she said quietly, "this is the deepest and most serious feeling of my life."

He put down his pipe again, leaned across the table, gripped her shoulders, released them. "I know I'm a man, but I don't understand. What is it that she gives you?"

"Tenderness," she answered after a moment. "And her own need for that from me."

"The physical relationship . . . surely can't be . . . much?"

She kept her face carefully expressionless. "Do you really want me to talk about that?"

"Diana, what if this doesn't work out. What then?"

She understood what he was asking, and she deliberated for some time over her answer. "I would look for it again. Without any hope that I could find it. As for where I would look—"

"Baby," he said, and she understood that he did want to know her answer. "There are a lot of beautiful people in this world. A lot of people who can give, who need . . . tenderness."

"Dad, why did you never remarry? Mother's been dead for thirty years."

He looked at her. "You're really comparing that . . . with this?"

"Yes. I am. When did you first know that you loved Mother? How long did it take you to love her? Was there ever another love to compare?"

He did not answer. They sat in silence.

She inhaled the ineffably sweet smell of orange blossoms from the yard next door. Finally she said, "You insisted on knowing." She added, trying to make her tone light, "You promised not to be disturbed."

Eyes moist with tears, he said softly, "You can't expect me to be happy about something with so much potential to hurt the most precious person in my life." He cleared his throat, stroked his goatee, and tried to smile. "But give your liberal democrat father a little time." He picked up the deck of cards, held it out to her. "In the meantime, cut for deal."

The day she was to call Lane she awoke refreshed from dreamless, uninterrupted sleep. Her vigil over, she went eagerly to her job.

That evening she called time service, and set her clock. She paced the apartment and then sat tensely at the desk in her living room, staring across the room at the clock, watching the hands creep toward seven o'clock.

Heart thudding, she dialed the number on the business card propped against the phone, the number engraved in her mind, pressing the area code and numbers carefully into the push buttons of the phone.

"Diana?" The phone had been picked up on the half-ring.

"I was going to try to sell you Arthur Murray dance lessons," Diana managed to say.

Lane's laughter was soft, warm. "Are you all right?"

"Yes. Are you?" She was trembling, with relief and joy.

"Fine. You sound . . . are you sure you're all right?"

"Yes, but you didn't make any allowance for that. All month I thought you might be sick or hurt and I wouldn't know—"

"I thought that too, about you. What have you been doing all month?"

"Waiting for it to pass."

"Did you . . . do any thinking?"

Diana said quietly, "I understand that you needed to give me the time. There wasn't much thinking to do."

There was a silence; Diana heard an exhaled breath blend with the hum of the telephone line. Then Lane said, "It's been . . . a long month. There are things we need to talk about now, things I want to say . . ."

Diana sat with her eyes squeezed shut, closing out everything but the tones and cadences of Lane's voice. She said, "It's so hard to talk on the phone. I wish — I wish I could see you."

"Can I take that as an invitation?" Lane's voice was low. "I can be there in two hours, a little after nine."

"Oh Lane yes." Diana felt her pulse in her throat.

"Western flight one-twenty-four. It lands at nine-ten at Burbank. Will you meet me?"

"I'll be there."

"Diana?"

"Yes, Lane?"

"Nothing," Lane said huskily, after a moment. "I'll see you in two hours." The phone clicked softly.

Diana looked dazedly around her apartment, went to the sofa and fluffed up the pillows, picked up magazines from the coffee table to tidy them.

Tonight she would be with Lane. With Lane.

She flung the magazines down and ran to the bathroom to run water for a bubble bath, thinking frantically about what she would wear to the airport.

Lane was the third passenger off the plane. Diana was blurrily aware that she wore a gray sweater and pants, a simply cut dark blue jacket; and then Lane's arms were around her, blonde hair was against her face.

"People hug at airports," Lane soon murmured against her ear, "but usually not for this long."

They released each other. Lane held her at arm's length. "Hello," she said.

"Hello." Diana gazed at her, still weak from the scent of her perfume. "You . . . look beautiful."

"Oh God so do you. I like . . . your dress."

Diana wore a white V-neck dress of light wool, her cross at her throat. "I thought I'd wear one for a change." She had meant her tone to be light, but she spoke self-consciously.

"I like it . . . very much." Lane's eyes were very blue, and shy. "Let's go, let's get away from all these people."

They made their way through the airport corridors. Diana said distractedly, "How was your flight?"

Lane shrugged, touched her arm briefly. "Fine, it was fine. Long."

"What about . . . Do you have luggage?"

"I have a toothbrush in my purse. I seem to have forgotten my pajamas."

"I suppose we can manage to keep you warm enough," Diana murmured.

Lane said, her voice amused, "I have to leave early. I need to be in court tomorrow. My flight's at seven. I'll get a cab."

"Of course you won't. I'm so glad you're here I wouldn't care if I had to take you back at three o'clock in the morning."

They got into Diana's car. "You're thinner," Lane said. "I thought it was the dress at first."

"I stopped taking birth control pills. I think it was partly that."

Lane reached to her, smoothed a lock of hair. "I'm glad you . . . You look good. Can you come to San Francisco for the weekend?"

"Yes, if you want," she answered with a tremor of shock. The weekend? Did she mean only the weekend?

"Yes, I want. Can you come tomorrow night? So we can have Friday, Saturday, Sunday nights together? I could take you to the airport early Monday morning. Is that all right?"

"Yes," Diana said. Was this what she had in mind? That they would only spend weekends together?

"I have a plane ticket for you."

"Everything's planned, isn't it." The words broke from her. "You were very sure I'd call, weren't you."

Lane laughed, ironic and rueful laughter. "Hardly. The best way I could get through the month was to assume you'd call, plan as if you would. The thought of you not calling—I couldn't think about that. And I've had years of practice not thinking about what I can't handle thinking about."

"Did you have dinner?" Diana asked, mollified, and still absorbing her answer.

"No, I've been too—Maybe there's a McDonald's around."

"All over the landscape. I'll fix you something. Is that okay?"

"I'd like that very much."

Diana closed and locked her apartment door, and Lane took off her jacket and tossed it over a chair, a gesture Diana liked. They came to each other.

Lane held Diana's face in her hands, and stared with unreadable eyes, her face tense and closed. Then one hand clasped Diana's shoulder, brushed down over her breasts. She pulled Diana to her. Her mouth was momentarily tender, then possessive, and her arms were a fully satisfying tightness.

For a long time there was Lane's body in Diana's arms. Diana finally murmured, caressing her shoulders, "You need to let me fix you some food."

"All right, but just something light. Show me your place, first."

An arm circling each other, they strolled around Diana's apartment. Lane examined her pictures and books, a few pieces of glass sculpture, the fine German clock given Diana by her father. When they went into the bedroom, Lane said, "You described it very well."

Diana stirred uncomfortably under her arm, warm as she remembered. Lane's laugh was gentle, teasing; she took Diana into her arms again. Some time later, her lips low in the V of Diana's dress, she murmured, "I really don't need any food."

Diana's eyes were closed in pleasure. "Yes you do," she said with effort, and stepped away, out of her arms. She pulled down Lane's sweater; her hands had been under it. "You need your strength."

"Do I," Lane said, reaching for her hand. "Are you planning to keep me up all night again?"

"Me? I'm the one?"

Holding hands, they went into the kitchen. Diana thought: She can't want us to be only part-time lovers, she just can't. She said, "It makes all the difference, knowing there'll be tomorrow night and nights after that, doesn't it?"

"Yes. All the difference."

Diana poured two glasses of wine. "How about a sandwich? A hamburger? Bacon and eggs? Some soup?" She smiled. "All three?"

"Do you have any chicken soup?"

Diana gazed at her with tenderness. "You're such a little kid about food. How about a hamburger with your soup?"

Lane grinned. "That sounds great."

Diana prepared food, and Lane sat at the breakfast bar sipping wine and watching her. "Have something with me," Lane said. "A little bowl of soup if you're not hungry. To keep me company."

"Okay," Diana said. "Bring me up to date about the group at the cabin."

"There's some news. Nearly as I can tell, Madge and Arthur are still status quo. Madge doesn't talk about it—I think she's still working on her courage. Millie's still Millie. Chris is seeing some man in her apartment building. According to Madge, Liz is upset that he's forty and Chris's forty-five. Not much wonder Chris managed never to marry all these years—first her mother and then her overbearing younger sister. The big news is George's blonde paramour." Lane grinned. "She's given him the boot."

"That *is* news. Has he called Liz?"

"Not so far. I don't think his pride is quite ready for that yet. But he's used the indirect approach—leaving all kinds of hints and messages with their two boys about how wonderful it was being married to Liz." Lane chuckled. "I think it'll work out, given time." She tasted her soup, bit into her hamburger. "Mmm, this is so good, Diana."

They sat together at the breakfast bar, Diana sipping a spoonful of soup occasionally, watching with pleasure as Lane ate her food. She picked up the plane ticket Lane had placed on the counter. "I didn't thank you for this," she said. "In fact I was hardly even—" She looked at the ticket and said in surprise, "This is first class."

"Right."

"To San Francisco?"

"I know it's not far," Lane said defensively, "but I want you to be comfortable."

"You're crazy," Diana said, shaking her head, very pleased. "But awfully nice."

"I have all kinds of things for you at my apartment. Every time I had an anxiety attack I went out and bought something to convince myself you'd call. I've got some pretty strange things. Four sweaters, all kinds of jewelry, a silver pen, a T-shirt that says I left my heart in San Francisco—"

Diana was laughing. "You crazy woman. I have something for you, too. But only one thing."

"What is it?"

"You'll see. The one really insane thing I did during the month was one Saturday I went over to Bullock's and smelled every bottle they had trying to find your perfume. I can't imagine what they must have thought. I just suddenly had to know what kind it was."

"Did you find it?"

"Nina Ricci."

"Right," Lane said, laughing. "That *is* crazy. The scent I associate with you doesn't come in a bottle." She looked at Diana with sparkling eyes. "I'm going to take you all over San Francisco. There's a restaurant in Sausalito . . . Will you wear that dress?"

"Yes, if you want. I have some others I think you might like."

Lane finished her food, sighing with contentment. She looked at Diana with very blue eyes. "What you bought me, can I have it now?"

"Sure," Diana said, smiling, swept again by tenderness. She went to the bedroom, and returned with a package.

Lane removed the ribbon and bright paper slowly, with the anticipation of a child. "Oh," she said, and lifted from the wrapping a volume of Emily Dickinson poems bound in dark red morocco leather, the title stamped in gold, with LANE CHRISTIANSON in gold letters in the lower corner of the front cover.

"I had it made for you," Diana said.

"It certainly doesn't look like a book club edition," Lane said, smiling, her hands caressing the leather, riffling the gold-edged pages. "What a beautiful thing to have. Thank you, Diana. I love it."

"I loved getting it for you."

"I've thought of so many places for us to go in San Francisco . . . But I won't want to let you out of bed. I'll have to depend on you to make me let go of you."

Diana heard, strongly felt, vulnerability. She said gently, "I won't want you to let me out of bed. I won't want to let go of you, either."

Their eyes held for a moment and then Lane smiled. Diana remembered quoting a line of poetry in a station wagon on a winding mountain road, and Lane turning to her with a similar smile that had pierced her with its intimacy and loveliness.

Lane said, "My apartment has a view of the Bay. The fog comes in at night, Diana, it's so beautiful. With enough time I think I could teach you to love my city."

"I know you could." Just ask me, she thought. Tell me how you feel and then ask me.

Lane said, "Let's pick out some music."

They sat on the floor in the living room, Lane leafing through the records in the cabinet. "We have to have *Pretty Eyes*," she said, pulling it out. "Tell me, would you consider living in San Francisco?"

"I think I'd like it." She was surprised by the calmness of her voice.

"It's colder than you're used to, but I could at least keep you warm at night."

"Is that a promise?" She glanced at Lane, her tone light, her heart pounding.

"A guarantee." Lane continued to flip through the records. "If you wanted to live in San Francisco, you wouldn't have to live with me if . . . if it was better. But I would — You wouldn't have to work. I'd take care of you."

"But I'd want us to take care of each other," Diana said slowly, stunned and dismayed. She asked in blunt desperation, "Lane, are you trying to be a man for me?"

Lane's hands paused on the records. She looked at the floor. "I suppose I am. You've always been with men. You're used to men."

"So are you."

"But I know now what I really want. Don't forget I had a month too, Diana. To think about this. All I care about is pleasing you as much as a man would."

Why don't you tell me how you *feel* about me, she thought. "Lane, what is it you think a man has ever given me that's so wonderful?"

"The obvious, to begin with."

"I take it you mean sexual apparatus. You know what I feel with you."

"The novelty might wear off."

"Novelty?" Calmly, but with a gathering of anger, Diana said, "You're not a novelty and what I feel is not a novelty. And there's nothing a man and woman do that we can't."

"I can't give you a child."

"Lane, I'm thirty-four. I've had two long-term male relationships. If I really wanted children, I'd have them by now."

"A man's strength, a man's protection."

"You're strong for me in every way I need. I feel more free to be what I am, I feel more protected with you than I ever have with anyone." She said vehemently, in heightening anger, "I'm not apologizing to you for being a woman. Don't apologize to me. Tell me this. If you'd met me while you were with Mark, would you have let me happen?"

After a lengthy pause Lane answered, "Much as I would have wanted you, it's difficult to say. I think you'd have taken me from Mark, but I'm not sure. There were other factors. Father was alive. And there was my own rather pitiful courage."

"If I had known *you* before this, there isn't a man in my life you couldn't have taken me from."

"You really don't know me very well, Diana. I don't know if I can take care of you . . . be enough for you in all the ways you'll need."

Diana thought: Take care of me? Be enough for me? Why doesn't she tell she *cares* for me? That's what I need to hear. She said, "Does anyone know that? I know you well enough. I know everything that matters. What kind of guarantees can any person give another? All I can be for you is what I am. I don't want you to be anything but the person you are."

As Lane continued to stare at the floor, Diana sighed and clenched her hands in frustration. "If I wanted a mannish woman I'd be attracted to Liz. God knows she's rough and mannish enough. I love imagining you in jeans and a shirt. I love the thought of you in a dress and high heels and jewelry."

"Every morning of the month," Lane said in a distant voice, "I woke up thinking I'd dreamed you, that you were the woman in my dreams and you'd never happened . . ."

Diana said furiously, racked with hurt, "You know what I think? You don't care about me at all. You want to be a man for me? You *are* like a man, and the worst kind. I'm just a woman's body to you. I'm just a dream figure, your faceless woman. Maybe I'm Carol. Maybe I'm just a symbol of the woman you really want to take to bed."

Lane stared at her, eyes wide with shock. "That's not true." Her voice was distorted with anguish. "Oh God that's not true. Carol and I were like children compared to this. I'm so afraid, Diana. I'm terrified of what I feel about you." Her voice had dropped to a barely audible whisper. Her lips trembled. "I don't know what I'll do if you hurt me."

"Lane, look at me." Diana reached to her, took her face in her hands. Lane's eyes were tightly shut. "Lane, look at me."

Gray-blue eyes, wet with tears, looked helplessly into hers. Diana said from the depths of her, "I'll never hurt you. Never."

Lane whispered, "I love you. I love you so much. I wanted to tell you so many times. I loved you from the first time I looked in your eyes in the encounter games. When you held my face in your hands like this. You're so gentle, so open to me, so warm. God, you're so warm. And when you cried in my arms I wanted to heal everything in you that hurt. Every time we touched I loved you. It was all I could do not to tell you. I couldn't tell you. I came so close, so close the last night when you talked to me and I made love to you . . . When we talked on the phone I almost told you . . . Oh God Diana, I love you so much."

Diana said, her voice breaking. "I love you. All I want in this world is to be with you."

Sometime later, clasping Lane tightly to her, she said in a voice that was muffled against Lane's sweater and still breaking slightly, "I was afraid too . . . afraid of you not loving me."

"I was afraid to ask for too much . . . afraid to ask for what I really want . . . to have you with me all the time."

They kissed again, without any gentleness at all. After a while Lane said, "Let's find music to make love to. All I want now is to make love to you."

"With me, not to me." Her head on Lane's shoulder, penetrated by the warmth of her arms, Diana said blissfully, "You make love with the person, not to them, when it's equal. Am I ever going to get you trained?"

"Maybe, but not tonight. It won't be equal tonight. You won't get a chance."

Diana kissed her ear lightly and felt Lane shiver. "I'm pretty sure I can make you change your mind," she said, smiling, and rested her head on Lane's shoulder again. She sighed and tightened her arms. "I think there are just too many problems with loving a woman. For instance, there's lipstick on your sweater."

"The stewardess will be so shocked," Lane murmured. "Will you come back with me in the morning? Take the day off and . . . be near me?"

"Yes. It would appear I'll be quitting anyway."

Lane stroked Diana's hair. "I can practice law anywhere . . . anywhere we want to live. If you'd prefer—"

"I can work anywhere, too. I think San Francisco would be a beautiful place for us to live."

"When did you know?"

"That I loved you? It was there all along, growing stronger. But consciously in the motel room. I knew I wanted to wake up every day of my life with you."

"It's fast, Diana, so fast for us to know . . . We'll have problems, Diana, being together."

"Yes, I know. But we'll be together. You asked me when we first made love how I knew how to touch you and I told you I just knew. I just know about this, too." Diana quoted,

> *"The Soul selects her own Society—*
> *Then—shuts the Door . . ."*

"I love you," Lane said.

Diana said, trying out the words, tasting them. "My dearest . . ."

A few of the publications of
THE NAIAD PRESS, INC.
P.O. Box 10543 • Tallahassee, Florida 32302
Phone (904) 539-5965
Toll-Free Order Number: 1-800-533-1973
Mail orders welcome. Please include 15% postage.
Write or call for our free catalog which also features an
incredible selection of lesbian videos.

FORTY LOVE by Diana Simmonds. 240 pp. Joyous, heart-warming romance.   ISBN 1-56280-171-6 $11.95

IN THE MOOD by Robbi Sommers. 112 pp. The queen of erotic tension!   ISBN 1-56280-172-4   11.95

SWIMMING CAT COVE by Lauren Douglas. 192 pp. 2nd Allison O'Neil Mystery.   ISBN 1-56280-168-6   11.95

THE LOVING LESBIAN by Claire McNab and Sharon Gedan. 240 pp. Explore the experiences that make lesbian love unique.
                                                    ISBN 1-56280-169-4   14.95

COURTED by Celia Cohen. 160 pp. Sparkling romantic encounter.   ISBN 1-56280-166-X   11.95

SEASONS OF THE HEART by Jackie Calhoun. 240 pp. Romance through the years.   ISBN 1-56280-167-8   11.95

K. C. BOMBER by Janet McClellan. 208 pp. 1st Tru North mystery.   ISBN 1-56280-157-0   11.95

LAST RITES by Tracey Richardson. 192 pp. 1st Stevie Houston mystery.   ISBN 1-56280-164-3   11.95

EMBRACE IN MOTION by Karin Kallmaker. 256 pp. A whirlwind love affair.   ISBN 1-56280-165-1   11.95

HOT CHECK by Peggy J. Herring. 192 pp. Will workaholic Alice fall for guitarist Ricky?   ISBN 1-56280-163-5   11.95

OLD TIES by Saxon Bennett. 176 pp. Can Cleo surrender to a passionate new love?   ISBN 1-56280-159-7   11.95

LOVE ON THE LINE by Laura DeHart Young. 176 pp. Will Stef win Kay's heart?   ISBN 1-56280-162-7 $11.95

DEVIL'S LEG CROSSING by Kaye Davis. 192 pp. 1st Maris Middleton mystery.   ISBN 1-56280-158-9   11.95

COSTA BRAVA by Marta Balletbo Coll. 144 pp. Read the book, see the movie!   ISBN 1-56280-153-8   11.95

MEETING MAGDALENE & OTHER STORIES by
Marilyn Freeman. 144 pp. Read the book, see the movie!
ISBN 1-56280-170-8   11.95

SECOND FIDDLE by Kate Calloway. 208 pp. P.I. Cassidy James'
second case.   ISBN 1-56280-169-6   11.95

LAUREL by Isabel Miller. 128 pp. By the author of the beloved
Patience and Sarah.   ISBN 1-56280-146-5   10.95

LOVE OR MONEY by Jackie Calhoun. 240 pp. The romance of
real life.   ISBN 1-56280-147-3   10.95

SMOKE AND MIRRORS by Pat Welch. 224 pp. 5th Helen Black
Mystery.   ISBN 1-56280-143-0   10.95

DANCING IN THE DARK edited by Barbara Grier & Christine
Cassidy. 272 pp. Erotic love stories by Naiad Press authors.
ISBN 1-56280-144-9   14.95

TIME AND TIME AGAIN by Catherine Ennis. 176 pp. Passionate
love affair.   ISBN 1-56280-145-7   10.95

PAXTON COURT by Diane Salvatore. 256 pp. Erotic and wickedly
funny contemporary tale about the business of learning to live
together.   ISBN 1-56280-114-7   10.95

INNER CIRCLE by Claire McNab. 208 pp. 8th Carol Ashton
Mystery.   ISBN 1-56280-135-X   10.95

LESBIAN SEX: AN ORAL HISTORY by Susan Johnson.
240 pp. Need we say more?   ISBN 1-56280-142-2   14.95

BABY, IT'S COLD by Jaye Maiman. 256 pp. 5th Robin Miller
Mystery.   ISBN 1-56280-141-4   19.95

WILD THINGS by Karin Kallmaker. 240 pp. By the undisputed
mistress of lesbian romance.   ISBN 1-56280-139-2   10.95

THE GIRL NEXT DOOR by Mindy Kaplan. 208 pp. Just what
you'd expect.   ISBN 1-56280-140-6   11.95

NOW AND THEN by Penny Hayes. 240 pp. Romance on the
westward journey.   ISBN 1-56280-121-X   11.95

HEART ON FIRE by Diana Simmonds. 176 pp. The romantic and
erotic rival of *Curious Wine.*   ISBN 1-56280-152-X   11.95

DEATH AT LAVENDER BAY by Lauren Wright Douglas. 208 pp.
1st Allison O'Neil Mystery.   ISBN 1-56280-085-X   11.95

YES I SAID YES I WILL by Judith McDaniel. 272 pp. Hot
romance by famous author.   ISBN 1-56280-138-4   11.95

FORBIDDEN FIRES by Margaret C. Anderson. Edited by Mathilda
Hills. 176 pp. Famous author's "unpublished" Lesbian romance.
ISBN 1-56280-123-6   21.95

SIDE TRACKS by Teresa Stores. 160 pp. Gender-bending
Lesbians on the road.   ISBN 1-56280-122-8   10.95

HOODED MURDER by Annette Van Dyke. 176 pp. 1st Jessie
Batelle Mystery.   ISBN 1-56280-134-1   10.95

WILDWOOD FLOWERS by Julia Watts. 208 pp. Hilarious and
heart-warming tale of true love.   ISBN 1-56280-127-9   10.95

NEVER SAY NEVER by Linda Hill. 224 pp. Rule #1: Never get involved
with . . .   ISBN 1-56280-126-0   10.95

THE SEARCH by Melanie McAllester. 240 pp. Exciting top cop
Tenny Mendoza case.   ISBN 1-56280-150-3   10.95

THE WISH LIST by Saxon Bennett. 192 pp. Romance through
the years.   ISBN 1-56280-125-2   10.95

FIRST IMPRESSIONS by Kate Calloway. 208 pp. P.I. Cassidy
James' first case.   ISBN 1-56280-133-3   10.95

OUT OF THE NIGHT by Kris Bruyer. 192 pp. Spine-tingling
thriller.   ISBN 1-56280-120-1   10.95

NORTHERN BLUE by Tracey Richardson. 224 pp. Police recruits
Miki & Miranda — passion in the line of fire. ISBN 1-56280-118-X 10.95

LOVE'S HARVEST by Peggy J. Herring. 176 pp. by the author of
Once More With Feeling.   ISBN 1-56280-117-1   10.95

THE COLOR OF WINTER by Lisa Shapiro. 208 pp. Romantic
love beyond your wildest dreams.   ISBN 1-56280-116-3   10.95

FAMILY SECRETS by Laura DeHart Young. 208 pp. Enthralling
romance and suspense.   ISBN 1-56280-119-8   10.95

INLAND PASSAGE by Jane Rule. 288 pp. Tales exploring conven-
tional & unconventional relationships.   ISBN 0-930044-56-8   10.95

DOUBLE BLUFF by Claire McNab. 208 pp. 7th Carol Ashton
Mystery.   ISBN 1-56280-096-5   10.95

BAR GIRLS by Lauran Hoffman. 176 pp. See the movie, read
the book!   ISBN 1-56280-115-5   10.95

THE FIRST TIME EVER edited by Barbara Grier & Christine
Cassidy. 272 pp. Love stories by Naiad Press authors.
                                           ISBN 1-56280-086-8   14.95

MISS PETTIBONE AND MISS McGRAW by Brenda Weathers.
208 pp. A charming ghostly love story.   ISBN 1-56280-151-1   10.95

CHANGES by Jackie Calhoun. 208 pp. Involved romance and
relationships.   ISBN 1-56280-083-3   10.95

FAIR PLAY by Rose Beecham. 256 pp. 3rd Amanda Valentine
Mystery.   ISBN 1-56280-081-7   10.95

PAYBACK by Celia Cohen. 176 pp. A gripping thriller of romance,
revenge and betrayal.   ISBN 1-56280-084-1   10.95

THE BEACH AFFAIR by Barbara Johnson. 224 pp. Sizzling
summer romance/mystery/intrigue.   ISBN 1-56280-090-6   10.95

GETTING THERE by Robbi Sommers. 192 pp. Nobody does it
like Robbi!   ISBN 1-56280-099-X   10.95

FINAL CUT by Lisa Haddock. 208 pp. 2nd Carmen Ramirez
Mystery.   ISBN 1-56280-088-4   10.95

FLASHPOINT by Katherine V. Forrest. 256 pp. A Lesbian
blockbuster!   ISBN 1-56280-079-5   11.95

CLAIRE OF THE MOON by Nicole Conn. Audio Book —Read
by Marianne Hyatt.   ISBN 1-56280-113-9   16.95

FOR LOVE AND FOR LIFE: INTIMATE PORTRAITS OF
LESBIAN COUPLES by Susan Johnson. 224 pp.
                                           ISBN 1-56280-091-4   14.95

DEVOTION by Mindy Kaplan. 192 pp. See the movie — read
the book!   ISBN 1-56280-093-0   10.95

SOMEONE TO WATCH by Jaye Maiman. 272 pp. 4th Robin
Miller Mystery.   ISBN 1-56280-095-7   10.95

GREENER THAN GRASS by Jennifer Fulton. 208 pp. A young
woman — a stranger in her bed.   ISBN 1-56280-092-2   10.95

TRAVELS WITH DIANA HUNTER by Regine Sands. Erotic
lesbian romp. Audio Book (2 cassettes)   ISBN 1-56280-107-4   16.95

CABIN FEVER by Carol Schmidt. 256 pp. Sizzling suspense
and passion.   ISBN 1-56280-089-1   10.95

THERE WILL BE NO GOODBYES by Laura DeHart Young. 192
pp. Romantic love, strength, and friendship. ISBN 1-56280-103-1   10.95

FAULTLINE by Sheila Ortiz Taylor. 144 pp. Joyous comic
lesbian novel.   ISBN 1-56280-108-2   9.95

OPEN HOUSE by Pat Welch. 176 pp. 4th Helen Black Mystery.
                                           ISBN 1-56280-102-3   10.95

ONCE MORE WITH FEELING by Peggy J. Herring. 240 pp.
Lighthearted, loving romantic adventure.   ISBN 1-56280-089-2   11.95

FOREVER by Evelyn Kennedy. 224 pp. Passionate romance — love
overcoming all obstacles.   ISBN 1-56280-094-9   10.95

WHISPERS by Kris Bruyer. 176 pp. Romantic ghost story
                                           ISBN 1-56280-082-5   10.95

NIGHT SONGS by Penny Mickelbury. 224 pp. 2nd Gianna Maglione
Mystery.   ISBN 1-56280-097-3   10.95

GETTING TO THE POINT by Teresa Stores. 256 pp. Classic
southern Lesbian novel.   ISBN 1-56280-100-7   10.95

PAINTED MOON by Karin Kallmaker. 224 pp. Delicious
Kallmaker romance.   ISBN 1-56280-075-2   11.95

THE MYSTERIOUS NAIAD edited by Katherine V. Forrest &
Barbara Grier. 320 pp. Love stories by Naiad Press authors.
                                           ISBN 1-56280-074-4   14.95

DAUGHTERS OF A CORAL DAWN by Katherine V. Forrest.
240 pp. Tenth Anniversay Edition.   ISBN 1-56280-104-X   11.95

BODY GUARD by Claire McNab. 208 pp. 6th Carol Ashton
Mystery.   ISBN 1-56280-073-6   11.95

CACTUS LOVE by Lee Lynch. 192 pp. Stories by the beloved
storyteller.   ISBN 1-56280-071-X   9.95

SECOND GUESS by Rose Beecham. 216 pp. 2nd Amanda Valentine
Mystery.   ISBN 1-56280-069-8   9.95

A RAGE OF MAIDENS by Lauren Wright Douglas. 240 pp. 6th Caitlin
Reece Mystery.   ISBN 1-56280-068-X   10.95

TRIPLE EXPOSURE by Jackie Calhoun. 224 pp. Romantic drama
involving many characters.   ISBN 1-56280-067-1   10.95

UP, UP AND AWAY by Catherine Ennis. 192 pp. Delightful
romance.   ISBN 1-56280-065-5   11.95

PERSONAL ADS by Robbi Sommers. 176 pp. Sizzling short
stories.   ISBN 1-56280-059-0   11.95

CROSSWORDS by Penny Sumner. 256 pp. 2nd Victoria Cross
Mystery.   ISBN 1-56280-064-7   9.95

SWEET CHERRY WINE by Carol Schmidt. 224 pp. A novel of
suspense.   ISBN 1-56280-063-9   9.95

CERTAIN SMILES by Dorothy Tell. 160 pp. Erotic short stories.
     ISBN 1-56280-066-3   9.95

EDITED OUT by Lisa Haddock. 224 pp. 1st Carmen Ramirez
Mystery.   ISBN 1-56280-077-9   9.95

WEDNESDAY NIGHTS by Camarin Grae. 288 pp. Sexy
adventure.   ISBN 1-56280-060-4   10.95

SMOKEY O by Celia Cohen. 176 pp. Relationships on the
playing field.   ISBN 1-56280-057-4   9.95

KATHLEEN O'DONALD by Penny Hayes. 256 pp. Rose and
Kathleen find each other and employment in 1909 NYC.
     ISBN 1-56280-070-1   9.95

STAYING HOME by Elisabeth Nonas. 256 pp. Molly and Alix
want a baby . . . or do they?   ISBN 1-56280-076-0   10.95

TRUE LOVE by Jennifer Fulton. 240 pp. Six lesbians searching
for love in all the "right" places.   ISBN 1-56280-035-3   10.95

KEEPING SECRETS by Penny Mickelbury. 208 pp. 1st Gianna
Maglione Mystery.   ISBN 1-56280-052-3   9.95

THE ROMANTIC NAIAD edited by Katherine V. Forrest &
Barbara Grier. 336 pp. Love stories by Naiad Press authors.
     ISBN 1-56280-054-X   14.95

UNDER MY SKIN by Jaye Maiman. 336 pp. 3rd Robin Miller
Mystery.   ISBN 1-56280-049-3.   10.95

CAR POOL by Karin Kallmaker. 272pp. Lesbians on wheels
and then some! ISBN 1-56280-048-5   10.95

NOT TELLING MOTHER: STORIES FROM A LIFE by Diane
Salvatore. 176 pp. Her 3rd novel. ISBN 1-56280-044-2   9.95

GOBLIN MARKET by Lauren Wright Douglas. 240pp. 5th Caitlin
Reece Mystery. ISBN 1-56280-047-7   10.95

LONG GOODBYES by Nikki Baker. 256 pp. 3rd Virginia Kelly
Mystery. ISBN 1-56280-042-6   9.95

FRIENDS AND LOVERS by Jackie Calhoun. 224 pp. Mid-
western Lesbian lives and loves. ISBN 1-56280-041-8   11.95

BEHIND CLOSED DOORS by Robbi Sommers. 192 pp. Hot,
erotic short stories. ISBN 1-56280-039-6   11.95

CLAIRE OF THE MOON by Nicole Conn. 192 pp. See the
movie — read the book! ISBN 1-56280-038-8   10.95

SILENT HEART by Claire McNab. 192 pp. Exotic Lesbian
romance. ISBN 1-56280-036-1   11.95

THE SPY IN QUESTION by Amanda Kyle Williams. 256 pp.
4th Madison McGuire Mystery. ISBN 1-56280-037-X   9.95

SAVING GRACE by Jennifer Fulton. 240 pp. Adventure and
romantic entanglement. ISBN 1-56280-051-5   10.95

CURIOUS WINE by Katherine V. Forrest. 176 pp. Tenth Anniversary Edition. The most popular contemporary Lesbian love story.
ISBN 1-56280-053-1   11.95
    Audio Book (2 cassettes) ISBN 1-56280-105-8   16.95

CHAUTAUQUA by Catherine Ennis. 192 pp. Exciting, romantic
adventure. ISBN 1-56280-032-9   9.95

A PROPER BURIAL by Pat Welch. 192 pp. 3rd Helen Black
Mystery. ISBN 1-56280-033-7   9.95

SILVERLAKE HEAT: A Novel of Suspense by Carol Schmidt.
240 pp. Rhonda is as hot as Laney's dreams. ISBN 1-56280-031-0   9.95

LOVE, ZENA BETH by Diane Salvatore. 224 pp. The most talked
about lesbian novel of the nineties! ISBN 1-56280-030-2   10.95

A DOORYARD FULL OF FLOWERS by Isabel Miller. 160 pp.
Stories incl. 2 sequels to *Patience and Sarah*. ISBN 1-56280-029-9   9.95

These are just a few of the many Naiad Press titles — we are the oldest and
largest lesbian/feminist publishing company in the world. We also offer an
enormous selection of lesbian video products. Please request a complete
catalog. We offer personal service; we encourage and welcome direct mail
orders from individuals who have limited access to bookstores carrying our
publications.

The Little Valley series

Ella Yoder and Aden Wengerd's wedding and their move to their dream house is set for June. The beautiful wedding quilt is almost finished when tragedy strikes and the life they'd planned together is demolished. *Why would God take my true love home?* Ella wonders.

With Aden gone, Ella's future is uncertain. Daniel, Aden's brother, decides to finish Aden and Ella's dream house. Should Ella sell the home and land? Or will she go against tradition and move in to the house alone?

When a very eligible bachelor calls, Ella faces family and community pressure to accept his courting. Torn between her heart and Amish expectations, Ella must choose...

Ella Yoder has moved into her dream house. Living alone for the first time, she ponders her options. *How will I make a living? How will I live without Aden? What will become of me?* Two would-be suitors soon make their intentions known, and Ella faces pressure to accept one of them.

Ella agrees to take care of Preacher Stutzman's three motherless girls. Her heart is touched by their love for her. Is their affection the answer for Ella's shattered heart? Does God want her to marry Ivan so she can be the mother his three children need? But there's the bishop's offer of marriage to consider...and the unusual option of staying single and living in the home Aden designed.

Ella loves the widower Ivan Stutzman's children. She is genuinely devoted to Ivan and keenly aware of his desire to propose, but her feelings stop just short of romance. Is her love for Ivan's children enough to make a marriage work?

When a handsome *Englisha* man seeks Ella out to ask about the Amish faith, Ella is wary but intrigued. She agrees to meet with him—but only with the bishop's approval. Soon Ella is torn between her devotion to Ivan and his children and her growing feelings for the *Englisha*. With dire consequences at stake, Ella must decide what her heart really wants, what God's will is for her, and whether she will stay true to her Amish heritage.